SARAH OF THE SLUMS

VICTORIAN ROMANCE

ELEONOR CORNISH

PUREREAD.COM

Copyright © 2024 PureRead Ltd

www.pureread.com

All rights reserved. No part of this publication may be reproduced, distributed or transmitted in any form or by any means, without prior written permission.

Publisher's Note: This is a work of fiction. Names, characters, places, and incidents are a product of the author's imagination. Locales and public names are sometimes used for atmospheric purposes. Any resemblance to actual people, living or dead, or to businesses, companies, events, institutions, or locales is completely coincidental.

CONTENTS

Dear reader, get ready for another great story...	1
Prologue	3
Chapter 1	9
Chapter 2	21
Chapter 3	39
Chapter 4	51
Chapter 5	64
Chapter 6	78
Chapter 7	99
Chapter 8	109
Chapter 9	121
Chapter 10	136
Epilogue	142
Have you read?	148
Love Victorian Christmas Saga Romance?	163
Our Gift To You	167

DEAR READER, GET READY FOR ANOTHER GREAT STORY...

A VICTORIAN ROMANCE

In this gripping historical romance, Sarah's resilience is tested, her heart torn between duty and desire.

Can she keep her family from unravelling, or will the bonds of blood prove to be her downfall?

Turn the page and let's find out...

PROLOGUE

There was a cry, a pained, piercing, awful cry that rose above even the relentless whining of the trapped pulleys and grinding gears of the machine.

The women gathered around the device began to shriek. Several took alarmed steps backwards, one ran right to the far end of the factory floor and cowered fearfully. Two of the older women, with missing digits on their hands, rallied themselves. They pushed down onto their hands and knees, peering into the dark beneath the machines and spying the body trapped within.

"Laura! Laura!" the women called out, but all they got in response was more screaming.

"Can you see her? Can you reach her?"

"I have no idea," one of the women said, pushing back up from under the machine, her face grim and stony. "She's flailing like mad under there and not listening to a word."

"Oh, God, please help us!"

The woman who had just pulled herself up frowned at the way her factory sisters stepped back from her. Only when she noticed the smear of blood staining her apron did she realise what had alarmed them. She looked back to the machine, eyes wide as she saw a visible pooling of dark red just beginning to trickle out onto the tiled floor by their feet.

"Hasn't anyone found the foreman yet!" Boys! boys! We need you under there, now, to help her out! Break the machine if you like, but we need to get her out—now!"

The ant-like workers ceased their usual labours and scurrying, moved in a mix of panic and uncertainty as they gathered around the growling and broken machine that had taken one of their own prisoner.

Laura Price.

The woman was a good enough worker, talkative and pleasant, though somewhat overbearing when it came to her children. If you got her started on that topic you were likely never to hear the end of it or get a word in edgewise. Any excuse Laura had to talk of her three gorgeous and wonderful boys she would take with barely concealed enthusiasm. The way she spoke of those three, anyone would think she was the proud mother of blessed saints. Though it was perfectly natural for a mother to dote upon her children and to think the world of them, Laura Price took it to excess. More than once, she had been reprimanded by the foreman for getting caught up in chatter when she should have been paying attention to the machine she operated in the textiles factory. Now, she was paying an even greater price for her carelessness.

Laura had just begun launching into another of her stories of her darling little ones' escapades when her machine had begun to jam and stall. Rather than wait for one of the nimble and slight bodied boys to come and crawl under the machine, Laura had decided to set herself to the task, pushing her head under to see what was the matter, all the while with a smile on her face. She was still to be heard talking about her boys when something went terribly wrong.

By the time the woman had been pulled out from the claws and dagger-like appendages of the broken-down machine, she looked like a victim of Jack the Ripper himself. Those who saw her screamed and the foreman had to almost beat the other women to return to their stations and continue work, or else mop up the mess of blood left on the floor.

She was borne on a crude stretcher made of linen sheets and carried awkwardly, by those women whose stomachs could stand the grizzly sight before them, into the foreman's office where they awaited a doctor.

"She'll be dead before anyone can even arrive to look at her! We should call a priest!"

"She's not dead yet. If anyone has a reason to fight for life, it is her. Got her four kids to look out for, and no woman is more attached to her children than she. You mark my words, she'll fight and cling to life for them."

"Four… I thought it was three?"

"She has the girl too. Never talks about her eldest as much as she does the boys."

The women attending the bloodied and unconscious Laura Price kept their conversation going as best they could. They needed a touchstone of normalcy, something wholesome to keep their minds steady as they tried to stem the bleeding that seemed to be coming from a hundred lacerations and cuts to Laura Price's lower body.

"How old?"

"What?" the eldest woman asked, not quite paying full attention as she mopped Laura's brow with a damp cloth.

"How old are her children… She's always going on about them, so I never really listen."

"Between five and eight for the boys, I think… the girl might be ten? Will be an awful blow for them if she doesn't make it through… No father about anymore."

"It'll be bad for them if she lives too," another woman chimed in, her words grim and pessimistic. "Just look at her. Even if she survives, she's never going to be moving again. I'm no doctor but I can tell you that for certain… I wouldn't want to survive this were I in her shoes."

"Four children left to care for a crippled mother… or a dead one… Whatever will become of them I ask you?"

CHAPTER 1

Sarah felt thoroughly out of place as she stood in Mr Edwards's office. As she waited for Mr Edwards's arrival, Sarah looked down at her own tired dress and felt thoroughly ashamed. She had come wearing her Sunday best for this meeting but even this didn't seem to be enough when facing the grandeur of Mr Edwards's factory office. As she considered the conversation to come, she wondered if she should look to apologise to the master for tainting the space in which she now stood so awed and humbled.

Everything in the room was both foreign and familiar to her all at once. She could identify every item in the room —chair, table, paper, pen, ink, books—but had never seen such commonplace items made to such ornate and luxurious standards. Every time her eyes moved to the floor, she became distracted by the rich detailed designs of the carpet rug that formed a neat box around the great table. It was deep and plush, the legs of the desk sunk into the material by a good half an inch. Needless to say, Sarah took great care not to stand anywhere near the edge of that magnificent, black-and-red patterned luxury.

She felt sure the office itself had to have its own dedicated attendant whose sole purpose in life was, hour by hour, to eradicate every mote of dust and speck of dirt that might invade the hallowed walls of the master's office.

Of course, even dressed in her Sunday best, Sarah had not expected to be dealing with the factory master himself that afternoon. She had expected to meet with the foreman, and that prospect alone had left her nervous enough. To meet with the owner added complexity and fearfulness to matters that Sarah despised. The matters she had come to discuss were distressing enough. The last thing she needed was the difficulty of trying to maintain her best decorum while pleading her case.

As a myriad of doubts and fears mingled with the awe-inspiring visions around her, Sarah Price felt her mind becoming thoroughly lost. Her private contemplation began to take over her senses, making her numb to the sounds of industry coming from outside the confines of the decadent space she stood in. Compared to the dreary factory floor with its ever-whirring machines and tired, expressionless workforce standing at their stations, this room was like stepping out of reality and into heaven.

And then reality brought her back with a jolt.

The door to the office opened, and Sarah jumped at the sudden intrusion on her thoughts. She turned to see a lady of the utmost refinement and poise enter into the room, moving over to a leather lounge chair that dominated the eastern wall. Her heeled shoes, hidden under the petticoats of her gently sashaying olive dress, set a rhythmic beat as she walked around the room, taking the longest route to reach the lounge chair. She moved right around the central desk, not caring to slip too close to Sarah as she walked. Sarah watched as the woman took her seat, wondering if the elegant lady had taken lessons in the art of sitting down. She sat with such precision, her back straight and poise perfect. It was hard to explain just what it was in her manner that was so impressive, but Sarah knew she would never see another woman take to a chair in quite so fashionable and artistic a manner ever again in her life.

A tapping sound from behind her brought Sarah's focus away from the woman before she could be accused of staring rudely. This time, the noise came not from shoes alone, but from the distinctive clack of a cane on the hardwood floor. Sarah straightened her back, rigid as a ruler. Though she wished to look on the master's face, she forced herself to stare straight ahead, eyes on the black leather chair ahead of her.

The man took off his hat, laying it and the cane on the right side of the desk and ruining the perfect symmetry of his neatly stacked papers and utensils. Sarah bowed her head respectfully as the man looked at her. Still, even with her eyes trained on the carpet, she noticed a few things. He was a younger man than Sarah had expected. His hair was light brown and his face round and a little chubby. He was by no means unhealthy, but he had that slight paunch that Sarah noticed on certain upper-class gentlemen on the rare instances she caught sight of them.

"I apologise for making you wait, Miss Lucas, but I was advised by the foreman that I should hear this young girl's case. A ghastly business."

"Oh, it is quite alright," the smart-looking lady returned in a voice whose every inflexion and uttered syllable seemed flawless.

"Now, you are Miss Laura Price, am I correct?" the gentleman asked, folding his arms across his chest as he looked at his visitor.

"It… It is actually Sarah Price, sir. Laura Price is my mother," Sarah corrected, fearing that she should perhaps have let the error stand rather than presume to correct the gentleman.

"Ah…yes, indeed," the man replied, cheeks flushing a little as he seemed to give a nervous glance to the woman opposite. "You have my deepest sympathies for the incident that saw your mother confined to her bed. I was most distressed to hear of it, and I insisted that I should be the one to review the matter and ensure your family were taken care of in this difficult and trying time. Tell me, is your mother recovering well? Will you send on my best wishes for her recovery?"

Sarah was humbled and, honestly, a little taken aback by the generous and caring spirit of Mr Edwards. Sarah had never heard her mother speak much of the factory owner, but no stories of him painted him as particularly giving in nature.

"I… I thank you for your concern, sir. I will pass on your good wishes to my mother… I am sure she will be most grateful to receive them," Sarah replied. Honestly, her mother would not care one jot what 'wishes' her employer had for her health, not unless Mr Edwards was also willing to pay for a better doctor to ease her pain. Still, she would not dare to speak so freely with the man. She needed his patronage and goodwill and counted her blessings that she had caught him in such good humour.

"Now, I have it on good authority from the foreman that you are looking to take over your mother's position at the factory. I will admit, we do not normally employ girls of your height and age for her position… Children, such as yourself, are best used in clearing the machinery when there is a clog or a break and so forth."

Sarah nodded, looking down at her own slender and delicate fingers that were even now wringing the fabric of her dress nervously. She was older than she looked, nigh on eleven, but had not grown quite as fast as other girls her age. She was sure the gentleman mistook her for eight or nine.

"I suppose, if I were to put you to work with the other children, there would be some issue regarding the pay."

"Y-Yes, sir," Sarah admitted, her face flushing redder still as she tried to negotiate with the man so completely superior to her in wealth and consequence. "My mother's income was enough to keep our family happy and content," Sarah assured, though to call their living 'content' was something of an exaggeration. "Unfortunately, now that Mother can no longer work and requires daily care at home, I must look to find work of comparable pay. I have younger brothers, but they are not yet old enough to work and must remain at home to look after our mother in her current state."

"Of course, of course… a most difficult time for your family indeed," Mr Edwards acknowledged. "And I want you to rest assured, Miss Price, that I shall do all within my power to look after you and your family at this distressing time."

"You will?" Sarah's eyes grew round in equal parts with shock and delight. She was at a loss to understand just what had put the man in such a generous mood. Still, she thought she had an inkling as to his motivations as she noticed his gaze fall routinely back to the very smart and beautiful Miss Lucas. The way he looked to her, it was almost as though he were seeking her approval. Sarah did not know much about the ways of love and courtship, but she knew enough to understand when a boy was going out of his way to impress someone. This was such a time. Miss Lucas, disinterested and aloof, was the clear object of Mr Edwards' affections and he was no doubt hoping a display of generosity would go some way to proving his worth. Sarah had no idea if his gambit was working. There was no outward sign or display from Miss Lucas to suggest she was paying the matter much attention. Then again, Sarah didn't care what Miss Lucas thought, just so long as the master was a good as his word in looking after her family.

"We shall look to put you into your mother's vacant position, Miss Price, and at the pay your family are accustomed to receiving. From time to time, though, you may still be called upon to go under the machines and see to any problems that arise, as would be expected of someone of your age."

"That is indeed most generous," Sarah said at once, not wishing to show the slightest hint of ingratitude. In truth, she might have preferred Mr Edwards to send a physician or perhaps give an extra payment to help look after her mother in the short term. But Sarah was a realist. For all her 'wishing' she knew she was lucky to be given even this much consideration by the factory owner. Had she dealt with the foreman, had Mr Edwards not been looking to impress the fair Miss Lucas, she could well have come out with much less for her troubles.

"Of course, I doubt you will be able to operate the machines as fast as your mother would have. Productivity in the factory will surely suffer as a result of this. But I believe it is my moral duty to care for those in my employ, even if it means taking a hit to my own pocket."

"A most generous gesture," Miss Lucas said, at last acknowledging the man's attempts to impress her. "I must say though, I do not think you should have much trouble from this little girl. Why, her manners and address are quite impeccable. Were she not dressed in such shabby raiment, I might easily believe her to be a maidservant in the making. I might even know of a place for her in my own home should she prove to be a swift learner."

Sarah looked at Miss Lucas and couldn't help but smile. What child could resist grinning at such a compliment? The thought of becoming a maid, too... such a position would pay much better than the factory, she was sure, and was doubtless less hazardous to one's health. Sarah was so taken aback, she could barely string two words together. It didn't help that she now wanted to accentuate her 'polite manner' yet further to continue impressing Mr Edwards' visitor.

"Thank you, ma'am," Sarah said, curtseying, perhaps a shade too dramatically. She opened her mouth to speak again but was quickly cut off by Mr Edwards.

"You are most generous, Miss Lucas, but let us not trouble ourselves too much with this matter." The man shot Sarah a look. It was only for a moment, a flickering suggestion of irritation that turned to a sycophantic smile as he looked back to his guest. "Miss Price will be more than taken care of and happy here in her mother's position. It is almost one o'clock and I would not wish to waste our day together any further with ferrying this girl to your home and explaining her situation to your parents. I am sure they would not want to be impositioned with a matter that is obviously mine alone to solve."

"As you choose," Miss Lucas replied with a casual shrug of her shoulders. Whatever interest she had taken in Sarah immediately vanished at Mr Edwards' words and Sarah cried inwardly to be denied the opportunity Miss Lucas seemed to be dangling in front of her for one fleeting moment. She forced the compliments and the maid's position from her mind, focussing fully on Mr Edwards again and trying not to let her disappointment show on her face.

"Well, Miss Price, if you will walk behind us, I will advise the foreman of my decision and he will handle the particulars of your new position."

Sarah swallowed back the disappointment she felt at the sudden change in atmosphere about her. Though she had thought Miss Lucas's words would be a boon to her cause, they seemed to have had almost the opposite effect. Now that Mr Edwards's 'generous deed' was in danger of being out classed and outdone, he seemed eager to put Sarah Price to one side and find some other way of proving his worth to the young woman in his company. It galled her to think that her mother's life-changing and crippling injuries, were nothing more to the man than fodder to be used in his attempts at courtship. It galled her, even more, to think that the master would get away with such callousness, that Sarah would continue to say please and thank you all the way to the foreman to secure what generosity she had been fortunate enough to secure from the man.

Quiet and demure, Sarah followed behind Mr Edwards and Miss Lucas, taking great care not to tread on the woman's expensive dress. Mr Edwards led them down to the factory floor where the foreman immediately came over and engaged in a brief discussion with the owner. Miss Lucas made a beeline straight for the door, no doubt uncomfortable in the heart of the factory. Sarah watched the proud, tall woman leave, heaving a wistful sigh as she thought of the opportunity that couldn't be.

"Miss Price! Over here!"

With Miss Lucas gone, the foreman showed no care as he hollered for her, having to compete with the incessant whir of the machines as he tried to grab her attention.

"I'll leave her in your capable hands," Mr Edwards said, patting the foreman on the shoulder and then walking away at a clipped pace, clearly eager to return to Miss

Lucas and continue his pursuit of her. He left the room without so much as a backward glance, no real care or interest in her at all. And still, Sarah knew she had to remain silent and grateful.

"Bad business, what happened to your mother," the foreman said, wasting no time as he marched up the aisles of machinery toward a vacant space. "Honestly, I'm surprised she was pulled out of the machines alive. The way she looked when she was taken out of here, I'm not sure her living was a blessing or a curse."

Sarah's lips pursed thin. The foreman had no tact whatsoever. Still, at least he wasn't trying to feign any compassion or interest in her.

"The boss says you're taking your mother's station and frankly I don't care to argue. I'll walk you through the basics now and you better take to the work like a fish to water. This factory runs on efficiency and a speedy production line. I know Mr Edwards is doing you a great service by letting you take your mother's spot here, but I guarantee I can convince him to take it all back if you aren't a quick learner."

"I understand," Sarah said somewhat robotically. She would not look to argue with the foreman. Whatever trials awaited her; she would simply have to rise to them. She could not afford to lose the money she would be bringing in to support her mother and her three brothers. The foreman could ask her to do the work standing on her head blindfolded and she would still give it her best shot if it meant keeping a roof over her family and food in their bellies.

Sarah listened as attentively as she could to the foreman, memorizing every instruction as she prepared to take over the work that had crippled her mother.

CHAPTER 2

Henry stood with arms folded and legs set squarely apart as he stared down the boy opposite him. The two groups of boys were at total odds with each other, each superior in their own way. For Henry, Walter and Robert, their pride came in their attire, markedly better quality and in better repair than the urchins standing in front of them. The other set of boys had height on their side and, in their childhood world, height made right. Henry had done his best trying to wrangle control of the group around him, making himself the tough big shot shouting orders on what games they should play, but he was quickly finding himself outclassed.

"You want to go and play games, go find a baby carriage and crawl into that," Jim Peterson sneered. "We don't have time to go playing games and running to our mommy every time you scrape your knee."

"Hey, we do not go running to our mother for anything," Robert insisted, stepping out from behind his brother to defend him.

"That's right," Henry said. "We stay out dawn till dusk, and do what we like, when we like. We don't need anyone looking out for us. So what if we play games from time to time, we just do what we want, when we want. Nothing wrong with that, is there?"

The taller boys looked to each other again, then looking to their leader to continue proceedings while they sat back and watched in amusement.

"Well, if you just do what you want when you want, there's nothing wrong with that," Jimmy said with a shrug. "How about we get some hot cross buns, then we can do whatever you want to do."

"Now, you're talking sense," Henry agreed with a smile, thinking he had won the argument.

"Of course, you're buying, right?" Jimmy said, pausing in his tracks. Everyone else followed suit with him, casting half expectant, half suspicious, looks at the three brothers.

"Paying? We don't have enough money to buy three buns between us, let alone share them with you," Henry said, putting a hand defensively over his trouser pockets.

"Well, what do you intend to do then? You know me and the boys can't afford anything. You really expect us to just sit and watch you three eating buns while we go hungry."

"What else can we do?" Henry asked, almost pleading.

"Didn't you just say you boys do what you want when you want. I thought that meant you at least had the nerve to take something when you can't afford it."

"Stealing?" Henry's voice cracked a little and Robert and Walter behind him seemed to shrink back a little further as they left their oldest brother to sort things out.

"Stealing!" Jimmy parroted back Henry's word, putting on a shrill nervous voice in mockery. "We're talking a few hot cross buns here, not the crown jewels. No baker's going to go chasing you down and abandoning his shop. All we need to do is make sure there aren't any bobbies around to chase after you."

"Oh yeah, and what'll you be doing? If you think it's so easy why don't you just go and get something for yourself?" Henry countered.

"Hey, it's different for us. We aren't cut from the same cloth as you, with your fancy, clean clothes. We'd be getting dirty looks the moment we got near that shop."

"Well…"

"Come on, Henry, be a pal," Jimmy said, moving in close and putting an encouraging arm around the boy. "Me and the boys will do our bit. We'll make sure no bobbies are prowling the lane when you go. We'll give you a nice and easy path… just so long as you don't mess up."

Henry looked to his brothers. Their conflicted faces helped him little. The looks on the older boys' faces were becoming more and more impatient, and Henry knew he had to make a decision fast.

The three brothers lingered for the longest while outside the baker's shop. They had already made several false starts, walking up to the front of the store and peering through the window at the selection of buns and bread on offer and then chickening out at the last moment and scurrying away to a side alley. Little Walter reminded his older brothers twice that Mr Richards, the baker, was a kind man and had often given them a little extra when they made a purchase. As time marched on and the other boys waiting for them grew impatient, the three brothers forced themselves into the store, hoping that chance and Mr Richard's goodwill would be enough to see them get what they needed without having to take a chance on robbing the man.

The boys moved exactly as they had discussed in the alley, with Walter front and centre. As the smallest and youngest of the Price boys, he was the one most likely to win the old baker's sympathy and come away with the prize they needed.

"Well, if it isn't little Robert, Walter and Henry. How is your mother keeping, boys?" the owner asked, wiping his hands off with an apron and sending a cloud of flour flying everywhere around him.

"She's... She's doing well," Walter began, his nervousness clearly showing through.

"Walter tries to look on the bright side, but it's not been good for us lately," Henry added, thinking on his toes. "Mother complains and moans all through the night... Our sister is out working the day through and we have nothing to feed ourselves on during the day..." He paused as he spoke, eyes studying the baker for any hint that he was winning the man over with tales of their troubles.

"Well, I'm sorry to hear that, boys," the man said. "Tell your mother I'll keep her in my prayers and assure your sister that I will happily keep any orders she needs aside for her. Even if the shop is closed when she finishes her work, I don't mind coming down and handing her order over to her."

"Oh... Yes, we'll tell her," Henry replied, unable to stop a frown from spreading over his face. Mr Richards had been generous enough in the past, why couldn't he be so now, when they truly needed it? It left the brothers with only one option and Henry nodded at the other two.

"We have...um... Could we have two hot cross buns please?" Walter asked, still struggling through his words as he dug into his pocket and pulled out a few pennies. His hands were visibly shaking, the coins jingling madly in his palm as he stared up at the shop keeper.

"Are you feeling well, Walter. You look like you're coming down with a fever there?"

Henry feared for the success of their operation and acted on instinct. Stood by the front window, where Mr Richards had laid out his loaves and wares for display, Henry feigned a trip. It wasn't much of a fall; still, he splayed his arms wide over the display, knocking over multiple loaves, rolls and buns across the bakery floor.

"Hey, watch it. What is up with you boys today? You should be glad you're in my store; another shop keeper might charge you for messing up their good work like that."

Henry looked past the irate baker to his two brothers, Robert moving behind the counter and grabbing as many hot cross buns as he could carry, not looking at all subtle. For all their planning on how they might obtain the sweet treats, not one of them had thought about how they would get the things out of the shop without being seen. Henry, watching from the shop front, felt his stomach knot and a cold sweat break out across his face as he watched his younger siblings struggle with the load they had procured. One errant bun atop the wobbling pyramid in Robert's arms fell away, alerting the baker, who turned round in time to see the treat rolling toward him.

"Hey! What do you think you're playing at?"

At once, the three brothers ran. Their only advantage against the man before them was in their numbers. Mr Richards didn't know which of them to grab first and ended up with none of them as each ducked, weaved and shot out of the bakery and onto the streets. And that was only the beginning of their troubles. Jimmy and the other boys may have been good as their word ensuring no bobbies came down the street, but there were still plenty of folk around who saw them sprint out onto the streets. At the words "Stop! Thieves!" Every woman and man around them became a potential threat.

Henry had to duck to avoid a strike from a gentleman's cane. Robert dropped several more of the buns from his arms as he swerved out of reach of an older woman who tried to collar him. Walter only got away at all because of his mouse-like height.

How long the boys had to run, none of them could say. In their childlike minds of gross exaggeration, they could have sworn they were chased across the whole city by sixty, maybe seventy people, bent on bringing them to justice. When they did finally find a quiet alley in which to hide and take stock of their situation, they were dismayed to find they had only managed to keep hold of four hot cross buns between them. Not even enough for half of Jimmy's gang of boys.

"Jimmy will be laughing at us for weeks," Henry groaned as he bit down on one of the sultana and cinnamon baked treats. Reasoning that they didn't have nearly enough for the other boys, the brothers had elected to eat the lot. It seemed like the right thing to do and a good way for them to get rid of the evidence.

As the sun began to set over the city, the three youths trudged homeward, more concerned about running into Jimmy and his boys again than Mr Richards or a Bobby. They moved through the streets slow and purposeful, winding their way into the narrow corners of the city where the houses were match-stick thin and one could not move without someone's elbow or a wall jostling them. Their home was on the top floor of an old house at the end of the street. Two other families shared the property, one for each floor of the house. Before the boys had even opened the front door and climbed the stairs to their apartment, they knew something was amiss. Two of the neighbours were lingering near their windows and excitedly pointing at the boys as they passed by. The way the woman and her daughter seemed to whisper so frantically, it was as if the Price Brothers had become the talk of the whole neighbourhood.

With bellies growling and legs demanding the comfort of their beds, the three continued on up the stairs to the top floor of the building. The door was closed, but Robert swore he heard a masculine voice coming from inside as they fished around their pockets for the single key they shared together.

∽

Sarah heard the door go and looked to her visitor. She had always known Mr Richards to be a kind and tolerant sort, but then she had never had to see the man after his shop had been robbed. No amount of apologies, promises of punishments, and severe reprimands, were enough to satisfy the baker and he insisted on staying until the brothers returned so he could see to their punishment himself. As the door opened and the three miscreants slunk inside, Sarah could see the guilt and terror written plainly of their grubby little faces.

"It's the baker man. Run!" Henry gave the order, but the hall stairs were too narrow for the three brothers to make a swift escape. Mr Richards had both Henry and Robert collared before they had even made it two steps back down and Walter was not the kind to run off on his own. Mr Richards dragged the two boys back into the room, throwing Robert and Henry roughly down to the ground. Sarah winced to watch her siblings so abused, but she was in no position to stop the baker. After what the boys had done, she'd consider them lucky if they came away with only a handful of welts and bruises. She knew that miscreants had been sent to prison and hard labour for just such a crime.

"Mr... Mr Richards... Please... They... They're, just young boys. I'm sure they didn't mean—"

Sarah looked to her mother, rushing over to the bed that had been put out in the middle of the room. Mother didn't move much anymore. Even sitting in bed was a struggle and accompanied by great pain throughout her ruined body. Still, the sight of her boys thrown to the floor by the enraged Mr Richards had her moving frantically. She coughed all the while, blood spattering from her lips and staining the bedsheets as she clamoured forward in her own awkward fashion.

"Mama, please, you mustn't. The doctor said—"

"—No! I can't have you hurting my boys! Please, Frank, I'll do anything."

There was hardly anything in the world that Mrs Price could give in return for leniency from the baker. Still, there was something in her desperate plea that stayed the baker's hand. He gazed down at the two lads on the floor, and then to little Walter who had backed away into the hall: too frightened to run, too frightened to help his brothers. A sigh escaped the man's lips and he pinched the bridge of his nose as he found some semblance of compassion and reason.

"Guess there's nothing to be gained from beating your nasty little brats. They've already grown up too wilful and full of sin to be worth correcting now. If they were my boys, I'd have had my wife beat the evil out of them with a belt years ago. Too late now."

"Thank you, sir," Mrs Price gasped, coughing and spluttering as Sarah coaxed her back into the proper position in her bed. "You must understand, it has been so hard for us since their father was taken, and my accident, their nerves are—"

"—Spare me your sad story, Mrs Price. What you've been through is no excuse for stealing. You mark my words. I'll want the money by the end of the week. Eight shillings for the damage and ruckus your boys caused or I will take it out of their hides."

"You'll have it, Mr Richards," Mrs Price assured between rasping coughs.

"You'd better. And after that, I don't want to see any of your brood near my door again, do I make myself clear?"

"Perfectly," Sarah said, rising from her mother's side and giving an apologetic bow.

Mr Richards cursed and stalked out the room, taking a moment to strike Walter across the head as he departed, sending the child off in a fit of crying.

"Well, it serves you right," Sarah yelled, hands balled into tiny fists as she let out her frustration. "Do you have any idea what you've put me through this afternoon? What did you think you were even doing robbing a man who knows your names and where you live? Now, thanks to you, we won't have the money to feed ourselves properly for the next month! And when I want to get bread I'm going to have to travel halfway across the city, I'm sure, once Mr Richards tells the other traders what you did."

"Now, Sarah, don't yell," Mrs Price cooed. The three boys recognised their mother's understanding, all-forgiving tone and darted to her bed. They took no care with her as they nestled in close, their hands grasping at her, causing the woman to flinch and wince in pain. It was always the same. The tension in Sarah's shoulders left her and she slouched against the wall, reaching out to close the door to their cramped little two-room dwelling.

"They should at least go without dinner tonight," Sarah reasoned.

"Nonsense. Are you really going to let your brothers go hungry? Don't you think they've suffered enough, being abused by that awful man?"

"But Mother, paying back Mr Richards will see us struggling for weeks. We won't eat properly again for months," Sarah protested.

"Then we will endure it all as a family," her mother said, showing a great deal of conviction for one so frail. "If one of us doesn't eat, none of us do."

Sarah rolled her eyes. She knew well enough that there was no arguing with her mother. If she tried to deny the boys their evening meal her mother would only kick up a fuss and refuse to eat herself. Ever since their father had been taken far too soon in life, Sarah had noticed the way her mother seemed to coddle her brothers with an affection that bordered on embarrassing. Even as the boys grew and their mischief became obvious to all, Mrs Price would find ways to defend them and excuse their behaviour. They were her precious boys, each of them a reminder and a shadow of the love she had lost all too soon. She was useless with them even before she had been crippled. But, at least in those days, Sarah had been at home to watch them and keep them from the worst of trouble. Now, Mother could do little else but let the terrors run feral through the streets during the day. Sarah had tried to convince her mother that Robert and Henry were old enough to work, but she wouldn't have it.

Sarah felt tears of frustration welling at the corners of her eyes as she watched her nightmare brothers clinging to their mother. Henry, in particular, wore a most irritating smirk on his face as he looked out at his older sister from his place of safety. Though Sarah didn't care to think of it, she knew in her heart that the boys would not be able to enjoy their mother's protection for much longer.

"I'm going out for some air," Sarah said at last. "I'll make dinner when I get back, but don't expect much, any of you," she warned.

Needing time alone to work off her frustrations, Sarah opened the front door again, stepping out onto the landing and slamming the door behind her so aggressively that it sent a small plume of dust drifting up from the skirting boards.

∽

That night, Sarah spent a long time sitting up in bed staring out the window to the waxing moon. It was hard to see its silver shimmer, and it seemed to be disappearing further behind the rooftops opposite. Out on the streets, Sarah could hear two men arguing, their voices slurred from drink. The sententious rumblings seemed to have no real purpose or importance, but Sarah listened anyway. Her mind was simply too alive and tightly wound to permit any relaxation or sleep. She should be feeling elated, proud and pleased with how things had been at the factory in securing her family's future, but that was overshadowed entirely by her brothers' actions at the baker's.

She stared over at the bed opposite, eyeing her mother as she lay quiet and still in the big bed that was now her whole world. She tried to banish the resentful feelings that had been bubbling inside of her all evening, but it was a hard thing. Her brothers had been her mother's treasures ever since Father's death, and it stung to see how nothing they could do would provoke her to anger. Where it would end, Sarah didn't even care to imagine. The freedoms and indulgences the boys had enjoyed throughout their life were steering them down a bad path. That they thought they could rob a baker who knew their name and address was proof of their growing hubris. Meanwhile, Sarah taking on responsibility for the whole family did not even merit more than a tired thank you from her mother.

Letting out an irate sigh, Sarah forced herself to lie down, whacking her pillow angrily to try and form it into a more comfortable shape. She closed her eyes, her body tense beneath the sheets and hands balled into fists. She willed herself to sleep but found her mind gathering pace all the more as she considered how many hours she had ahead before she would have to get up and go to work.

A sound of groaning in the dark forced Sarah's eyes open again. She moved mechanically, pulling up on to her feet and walking across the room to her mother's bedside. She went down onto her knees, pulling out the bedpan ready in case.

"Mother... Mother, do you need something?" Sarah asked, putting a hand tentatively on her arm.

"Just... Just a tickle in the throat. Water, please."

Sarah put down the bedpan and turned to the side table. Filling the pewter cup with water, she let the cup be for a moment and helped lift her mother into a sitting position. The action brought all too familiar groans of pain, with her mother's hand grasping her arm tightly as she struggled to endure even these smallest of movements. Sarah looked to keep her steady as she propped up the pillows, only bringing the water to her mother's lips when she was sure she was secure.

"I can hear you tossing and turning over in the corner, you know," Mrs Price said as Sarah gently pressed the liquid to her lips. She took gentle sips, but even these agitated her and caused her to cough, Sarah quickly replacing the cup with a cloth. Only when her mother calmed did she look to address her question.

"It's been a long day," Sarah said, not caring to confide her true feelings.

"Don't give me that, girl, you've worn a fixed frown on your face ever since that baker left us this afternoon. If I didn't know better, I would swear you actually wished that man had laid his dirty hands on your brothers, for shame."

"Of course I don't wish that," Sarah snapped, carrying on with her work and wiping her mother's mouth and chin. When she drew away again, she felt a lump growing in her throat as her mother fixed her with a look in the dark. "I honestly don't want anyone to do harm to my brothers," she assured again. "Still, I wish you would not let them get away with so much. Robert and Henry are old enough to work and Walter should be at home with you."

"Now, you know I do not want my boys to lose the best years of their lives. I did not ask you to work until I had to," Mrs Price returned.

"And I was seven, Mother," Sarah reminded.

"But you had your father during those years," her mother reminded. "You do not realise what an advantage that was for you. Those poor boys, well, Walter doesn't even remember his father's face."

They were familiar arguments Sarah had heard before, yet another reason why she didn't want to waste her breath on the matter. Her mother continued on anyway.

"Remember, Sarah, when you are older, if you are lucky, you will be supported by a man who will look after you and keep you in comfort and peace just as your father once kept me. The boys, though, when they grow up, will have to work as hard as your father did to get by."

"Yes, Mother," Sarah replied in a manner that let her know she was no longer truly listening.

"You know, dear, I'm not long for the world."

"Don't speak like that," Sarah ordered, her voice curt and sharp.

"It's the truth," Mrs Price insisted, letting herself ease back down into the pillows. "It won't be long, and you will only have your brothers left. Maybe then you will come to cherish them the way I do... Understand how important the ties that bind really are."

Sarah made a noncommittal sound in the dark, her lack of an answer giving her mother cause to sit up a little taller.

"Now, you listen to me, young lady... I don't know where this spiteful attitude has come from, but you will look after your brothers when I'm gone, won't you? It's your duty as their sister and also my dying wish."

"Enough about dying," Sarah said, trying to force her mother to lie down so she could return to her bed. Mrs Price didn't let her, reaching out and gripping her daughter's arm. "I want you to promise me, Sarah. Promise me you'll look after those boys. There will come a time where you'll be glad you did so—where they will support you just as you support them now."

"I... I will, Mother," Sarah assured. She spoke the words primarily to convince her mother to let go and calm down. Still, as the young girl returned to her bed, something in her mother's words undeniably stuck to her. She didn't know why. Perhaps it was the urgency with which she had pleaded with her, or, maybe, it was the knowledge that her mother knew her time left with her family was drawing to a close. Whatever the truth, Sarah felt some renewed will to overlook her brothers' transgressions, to do her best for them despite their mischief. After all, when her mother was gone, what else would she have?

CHAPTER 3

Somewhere deep within the dark of the gears and pulleys, something had jammed and the whole system was backing up as a result. The foreman was casting irate glances and the other ladies stood back as the machine became a screeching, pained animal, ready to lash out at any that came too close. And Sarah was the one expected to tend to the wounded and angered beast. She lay on her stomach, staring into the dark ahead of her like some caver preparing for an expedition into an unknown dark tunnel. Except, Sarah was no caver and she had no desire for such adventures. As she listened to the demonic noises coming from inside the machinery all she could think of was her mother, the scars that riddled her body after the accident, her mangled legs that were rendered useless forever. Sarah had visions of herself laid out in bed, condemned to a slow and agonising existence of pain and boredom as she too waited for death as her mother did.

"Come on! What's going on here; what's the holdup?" The foreman marched over and Sarah glanced at his polished shoes as he came to a halt before her. "A fat lot of good you're doing lying down on the floor staring at the machine. This isn't nap time. Get in there and sort out the problem... Must be a fabric jam again. Get it before any of the gears break apart!"

The foreman was irate, shouting, but still, Sarah did not move. Though he was a fearsome and foreboding man, she feared the machines more. Even if the foreman were to take her into the office and beat her for laziness, there was no earthly way he could inflict on her the kind of injuries the unfeeling machinery was capable of dispensing.

"Did you hear me, Miss Price? Mr Edwards gave you a golden opportunity here and you are spitting in his face by cowering there. If you are not going to get in there and sort out that mess you've made, then you can feel free to walk out the door. I do not need some snivelling charity case squandering the master's money and wasting my time."

"I... I can't do it," Sarah snivelled, her eyes brimming with tears as she continued to stare into the dark beneath the machinery. She knew what her refusal meant, knew she was condemning herself and her family to destitution and perhaps even the workhouse. Still, the power of self-preservation was too strong and she just could not bring herself to crawl into the tangle of gears and pulleys and give up her body to the whims of the same machine that had crippled her mother.

"For the love of..." The foreman whistled and a boy in grubby clothes and about half Sarah's size ran over. The foreman casually kicked Sarah in the ribs, prompting her to push up onto her feet and let the boy through. The child was no older than five, she guessed, the same as Walter. Her cheeks burned with embarrassment and shame as the boy pushed straight down onto his belly and slid, grub-like, beneath the machinery without showing an ounce of fear. Once his little feet disappeared out of sight, Sarah turned away, not wanting to watch in case the machine took the boy as another sacrifice to its capricious whims.

"You can forget about finishing up the day," the foreman said, pulling alongside Sarah and folding his arms. She realised immediately there was to be no beating or even a raised voice from the man. As far as he was concerned, Sarah was out and he didn't need to waste his voice or energy looking to correct her.

"Sir, please... My mother is—"

"—Not my concern," the foreman snapped back. "I'm not running a charity here, Miss Price. If you're looking for charity, go and plead your case to the parish. And don't think Mr Edwards will come to your rescue, either."

"But sir, I can... I can do this," Sarah said, mustering her courage for a promise she wasn't even sure she could keep. "The next time the machines break down, I swear I will do better. I just need... Just need to..."

"It's too late now," the foreman said. "To be honest I was coming over to fetch you before the machines broke down. There's a bobby out in the offices wants to talk to you. Seems your brothers have gotten themselves into some trouble, and I will not have Mr Edwards's name or the reputation of this factory tarnished by keeping criminals in our employ."

"A bobby?" Sarah turned and looked to the foreman, forgetting all about the machine, her job and her fears for the future. All she could do was ask herself the question, what had her brothers done now?

Led out into the factory's front office, Sarah stiffened as she found a man in the dark blue uniform of the law, sitting on a bench. He had a thick brown moustache and a head of short, curly hair. His eyes were sharp and narrow, and his lip pulled into a worrisome scowl as he took in Sarah.

Picking up his hat and holding it under the crook of his arm, the officer stood and took three smart steps forward. "This is the girl, then?"

"Yes, sir," the foreman said with a gruff nod. "Feel free to take all the time you need with her; she isn't welcome back in the factory now anyway."

The officer shot Sarah a judgemental glance, raising a brow as though he expected such a report. "Well, well, seems I'm dealing with an entire brood of bad apples."

"H-how can I help you, sir?" Sarah asked, trying to maintain a polite composure.

"Your brothers are Walter, Robert and Henry Price, correct?"

"Y-yes, sir," Sarah said with a nod. "What has happened to them?" Though it was the worst thing imaginable to think for one's own siblings, Sarah prayed the three little troublemakers had been victims of an attack or accident. The last thing she needed was for any of them to have been caught on the wrong side of the law.

"Miss Price, your brothers were caught trying to pull a job on a fishmonger, out near the river. Seems they were working with a group of boys a little older than them. We've seen their type of game before. Your brothers ran a distraction while the older youths slipped round the back of the vendor's stall and took his lockbox."

"They didn't... After Mr Richards?" Sarah's mouth was agape and she shook her head in disbelief. How could they have been so stupid, and after being caught by Mr Richards only a few weeks before?

"I take it then you know of your brothers' crimes? If you've been encouraging their thievery then you and your whole family will be hauled to the magistrates along with them."

"What, no! No, that is not what I meant at all, sir," Sarah assured, putting up her hands and shaking her head more vehemently than before. "Please, my mother is very ill, left crippled from an accident in this very factory. I have been working here in her place, and it has left no time for me to watch my brothers. They... They must have fallen in with a bad crowd, but they have never acted this way before."

"Idle hands are the devil's plaything," the officer observed, straightening up and taking a deep breath that swelled his ample chest beneath his uniform. "Your brothers are what, eight, seven and six?"

"Walter is only five," Sarah corrected, though she knew the distinction mattered little.

"All three of them could be out working instead of running around the streets like motherless urchins."

Sarah bit her bottom lip and stared down at the policeman's shoes. She wouldn't answer back, but she felt like pointing out that the three were as good as motherless, all things considered. "What will become of them... Of us?" Sarah asked, recognising that she too could likely end up punished in equal part for her brothers' crimes.

"Seeing as though your services are no longer required here at the factory, I think you have time enough to walk me to your home. I want to see this mother of yours... I'll be interested to see if the woman is as bedridden as you claim or if this is just another ruse you're using to milk sympathy off unsuspecting folk."

"Oh no, sir. Mother is indeed gravely ill. I... I don't think it would be good for her to hear what has happened to the boys. She'd be beside herself with worry." Sarah still remembered the agitated way mother had tried to pull herself out of bed when the baker had come marching in with threats. How much worse would it be for a bobby to come marching in and telling her that her beloved boys were being held in cells and perhaps bound for prison. She looked up into the officer's eyes, hoping for some sign of understanding or sympathy. But there was none to be had.

∽

Though she stood at the door to her own home, Sarah felt the odd need to knock on the door and announce herself to her mother. Things would be bad enough with the officer coming in and the news that needed to be broken. She had to at least try and soften the blow, ensure her mother was at least in some way prepared for what was to come.

"Mother... It's me, Sarah. I've... I've got some bad news, I'm afraid. There was an incident in work and... And the boys, well they've... They've..."

Sarah could not find the words. She bit her lip, her fingers fidgeting with the fabric of her dress, twisting it in her hands as she tried to think of some way she could explain herself. The officer behind her had no time for it.

"Come on, I don't have all day," the man said, pushing the door wide open and stepping inside as if he was raiding some thieves' den. "Listen up in here, I'm constable Thomas Cooper and I'm... Oh no!"

At first Sarah didn't know what was the matter. The officer who had stepped in so full of bravado and confidence was stopped in his tracks, turning about and gagging as he stepped back into the hallway. Sarah frowned as she tried to look past him, not immediately understanding what had caused his change in demeanour. He might have caught her mother while she was struggling to use the chamber pot. Those few who had been forced to see her injuries in any detail had their stomachs turned by the sight and so it was understandable that the constable might have had some difficulty looking at her. Still, it surprised her when the man turned back into the hallway and closed the door behind him.

For the first time since she had met the officer, Sarah detected some hint of concern or pity in his eyes. He bent down onto one knee, drawing himself to her eye level, but casting a nervous look back to the closed door behind him.

"Are you quite sure this is your address?"

"Well, yes, of course it is."

"And your mother was alive and well when you left for work this morning?"

Sarah's face grew stony and she had the oddest feeling come over her as she seemed to understand just which way the conversation was leaning. Her mother was dead. It felt like it should come as a shock, that she should be moved by grief and burst into tears in an instant, but she did not. In a strange, almost horrible, kind of way, Sarah felt the strangest feeling of relief. She felt relief that her mother would not have to learn that she had lost the job they needed to get by. She was relieved she wasn't around to hear of her boys being arrested or brought to agitated panic by the officer who threatened them with the workhouse or worse. The doctor had warned from the first that she was not long for the world, even with the best of care. Death was a matter of when and not if, and there was the strangest feeling of peace to know that her mother had at last found rest, that she had found it before she could witness her children's lives crumble to ruin before her tired eyes.

"Perhaps... Perhaps you had better wait downstairs," the officer said, his voice strangely gentle now. "I will look things over here and come to collect you in a little while."

Sarah trudged down the stairs, leaving the officer alone to deal with her mother. She was glad of it. She did not want to see her mother lying limp and lifeless in her bed. She feared such a sight would bring the loss home to her, overwhelm her in a way she could ill afford. Sarah needed her wits about her and her mind sharp to navigate whatever was to come next.

Out on the street, Sarah paced back and forth, turning over in her mind what might happen for her and her brothers now. There were no certainties. Robert, Henry and Walter were held in police custody and their fate hung in the balance. If they were lucky, their mother's death might stand in their favour. It had already softened the officer who had come to her workplace. Even if the event were to spare them the magistrate or workhouse, there was the question of where they would go next.

As she paced the street back and forth, winding a lock of her brown hair between her fingers, she tried to remember the name of her uncle. She had not seen the man during her entire life to the best of her knowledge, but she was confident the man was alive and could be found somewhere in the world. She even suspected he lived in London, but just never cared to visit his sister or know his niece and nephews. Her mother's maiden name was Timpson, and Sarah felt like he might have been called James. If she was lucky, her mother had kept some papers or the parish record books could help her find the man who was most suited to become their guardian.

And what if her brothers found no leniency from the law? That thought sent a shudder through Sarah. She had lost her mother already today; she did not wish to lose her brothers as well and be left all alone. All of a sudden, she understood what her mother had tried to say when she warned Sarah that one day she would be thankful for her siblings, that the ties that bind are truly the ties that matter.

Her mind whirling a mile a minute, Sarah almost didn't notice the bobby emerge from her house, his face grim and his head hung low. She only noticed him after finishing another lap of the street. She paused in place, not sure of what she should do, how she should be with the man who earlier in the day had been treating her like a common criminal. She moved toward the man, casting nervous glances as she tried to decipher his mood and feeling.

"What is going to happen now?" Sarah asked, cutting to the heart of the matter. "Are you going to send my brothers and me to the workhouse?"

The officer looked down at her, lip curling as though he was chewing the idea over in his head. It felt like the man was still very much on the fence about how to proceed: his sympathy for Sarah contrasting with his desire to punish her brothers.

"Do you have any relatives who can take responsibility for you?"

"We have an uncle," Sarah said at once. "I... I think his name is James Timpson."

"Perhaps this relative might prove a better influence on your brothers and keep them out of mischief. Looking at the situation up there... I can tell your mother didn't have the time to teach them right from wrong."

"It was most hard on her," Sarah said, not bothering to mention that her mother had never cared to control her boys even before she had lost the use of her lower body.

"Well, we shall see if we can find this uncle of yours. If he'll take you in, maybe I can see my way to turning a blind eye to your brothers, for today."

"If I can be of any help, please tell me what I can do," Sarah said. She had no idea what kind of man her uncle was, but if he could offer her a roof over their heads and instill some measure of discipline in the boys, then maybe this day of tragedy and misfortune could yet be turned into something positive.

CHAPTER 4

Sarah stood in plush surroundings, admiring the finery of the office room where she waited for the master of the house to see her. The thick, red carpet, the sweeping oak desk with its neatly ordered papers, the well-stocked library of books behind: it took her back to that dim memory of the factory offices where she had pleaded for her mother's job after the accident.

So many years ago, now.

Sarah had grown up and she liked to believe she had grown up well. There had been hardships and difficulties: life with an uncle who did not care for her or his nephews' presence had presented its own set of challenges, but Sarah had risen to meet them all, each in their turn, and emerged from the other side as exactly the kind of woman she wanted to be all those years ago in Mr Edwards's factory offices.

Her uncle, Mr Timpson, accepted his role as guardian without complaint. He demanded Sarah and her brothers work to earn their keep but was not above using his influence to help them get ahead and find suitable positions befitting their skills. This had been easiest on Sarah who was already accustomed to the rigours of work by the time she entered her uncle's care. Sensible to her fears of machinery and factories, Mr Timpson had found Sarah work, first in a tailor's shop that specialised in handmade suits, but then later in servants' positions for various friends who needed the extra help. He looked to her education, too, raising the bar of her knowledge so that Sarah could now even entertain thoughts of one day becoming a governess if she continued down the straight and narrow path her uncle had forged for her.

Mr Timpson's generosity did not come free though. In return for his aid and the lessons he paid for, he demanded Sarah pay him back with interest. She was an investment, a promising investment that her uncle was confident to sink his finances into. He was hardly wealthy, little more than a bookkeeper to a firm. Still, he had developed a knack for recognising how to invest his limited fortunes wisely and safely and, as such, had always been able to live beyond what might be expected for a man of his profession.

Of course, Mr Timpson never took punts on causes he did not believe in and the opportunities delivered to Sarah were never extended to her younger brothers. Their relationship with their maternal uncle had turned sour within days of their entering his home and had never recovered. Used, as they were, to their mother's indulgent nature; it came as a shock to all three boys when their uncle locked them out of the house one night for running off into the streets to play when he had expressly ordered them to stay inside and clean.

While Sarah worked hard and was rewarded in kind, her brothers opted for a different path. Unable to forget the rose-tinted past they remembered; they labelled their uncle as a fiendish tyrant after having only spent the first months in his care. They fought him at every turn, forcing their uncle to use ever-stricter punishments to assert his control. It was a testament to the boys' delusional minds that they held onto their defiance as long as they did: convinced that one day they would win out and Mr Timpson would give them all the freedom and luxuries their mother had indulged them with in times past. So many of their early arguments with their uncle were accompanied by the useless phrase 'but mother would always let us.' This argument was in turn followed by their uncle's reminder that he was not their mother nor cared one jot what she allowed to pass in her house.

Needless to say, the difference in situation at Mr Timpson's home was hard on Sarah's relationship with her brothers. They began to resent her in the same way she had once resented them, thinking her a traitor or lackey of their uncle's. Sarah had never forgotten her promise to her mother. She truly did all she could to ensure the ties that bound her to her siblings were not broken by her uncle's different attitudes and treatment. She even used what limited goodwill and trust she had gained with the man to intercede with him on her brothers' behalf on more than one occasion. Though Henry, Robert and Walter never knew it, their stubbornness and lazy attitude to life had almost seen them thrown out onto the streets many times in the years they had stayed under their uncle's roof. Only Sarah's offer to add further interest onto the ongoing ledger her uncle was keeping to her name saved them from such sudden eviction. In the end though, the boys chose to leave of their own accord.

Fed up with their uncle's rules and unfair treatment, the three brothers moved out as soon as they had enough work and money between them to afford a shabby one-room home in one of London's back alley rookeries. Their uncle did nothing to dissuade the young men. He was glad to be rid of them. They were a drain on his finances; dead weight he needed to cast off at the earliest opportunity. After they took their leave, Mr Timpson counselled Sarah that she would be better off leaving the boys to their fates and concentrate on her own work and path. It was advice Sarah could not heed, and she made a point of going out to visit her brothers every few weeks, her promise to her mother demanding she at least check to be sure they were keeping a roof over their heads and earning enough to eat. To her relief, though the inseparable trio never seemed able to scrape enough together to raise themselves even to the level of comfort they had known as boys, they earned just enough to get by.

So much had changed since that day back in Mr Edwards's factory offices, and Sarah felt her chest swell with no small amount of pride as she let herself appreciate for a moment the gains she had made. Though the prim and fancy Miss Lucas would most certainly never remember her, Sarah wished she could revisit with that woman from long ago and show her what she had become. Miss Lucas had predicted she could become more than a simple factory girl, and now Sarah found herself in an interview to become housekeeper to a fine gentleman of London's West End.

The door opened and Sarah straightened up, clasping her hands together as she waited, eyes forward, for her prospective employer to look her over. She kept her chin high, proud but not aloof, and her warm brown eyes studied the man as he moved to his chair, interested to get a read on the man she had been hearing such good things about from her uncle and friend.

Mr Ralph Morgan had garnered a reputation in London as an employer comparable to Sarah's own record as an employee. The man's name was synonymous with a fair wage, generosity and genuine care and compassion for those who worked under him. The man kept several businesses and Sarah had been encouraged to apply for positions in several when opportunities arose.

Competition for such places was, however, fierce. When word of a fair and even-handed employer worked its way around the streets of London it was only natural that people would fight fiercely to obtain work with such a man.

On each occasion hitherto, when Sarah had tried to find work in any of the man's businesses, she recalled having to queue for hours for an interview, almost always met by some foreman, senior housekeeper or trusted employee who would conduct a startlingly fast interview on their master's behalf before showing her the door. That she stood now, not before some underling but Mr Morgan himself, and in his own home, was yet another source of pride for the ambitious young girl. Even if she were unsuccessful in her interview, there was much to boast of in having been granted an audience.

From what Sarah had been told through the gossip of friends and co-workers, Mr Morgan was very easy on the eye and an attractive prospect to any woman in more than one way. As Sarah understood it, any man who made an attractive income was made more attractive in body to her friends and so she had paid the rumours little mind. However, as she took her first look at Mr Morgan, she had to own that he was quite striking in his looks. His hair was short and dark, with thick eyebrows cresting dark green eyes. He was somewhat rakish in his physique, trim and healthy. Better that than the often-overweight gentlemen and ladies who tottered around and lived large, quite literally, from their wealth. Mr Morgan was well-groomed too, his pleasingly sculpted jaw free of stubble and shaved perfectly smooth. Best of all though was his smile.

Many gentlemen did not make the effort to smile at servants, even those whose company they enjoyed. So many interviews had been conducted under withering, sceptical gazes, some of Sarah's employers never looking to share a kind word with her until she had been with them at least a week and proven her worth to them. Mr Morgan dispensed with those kinds of observances, fixing Sarah with a most pleasing and generous smile as he took a turn about the room, inspecting her from all sides.

"My, when my friend mentioned he knew a woman who would make an ideal housekeeper, he neglected to tell me that she would be so fair of face."

Sarah's eyes widened slightly and a rose blush coloured her pale cheeks. Though normally the pinnacle of poise and calm, she was turned back to a time of a young girl, drunk on stories of knights in shining armour and fairy tales of true love with a handsome prince by the attractive man's words. Sarah had to work hard to prevent her hands from fidgeting or her smile from spreading too far across her face and leaving her looking ridiculous.

"Pray, how old are you, Miss Price?" Mr Morgan asked as he pulled out a chair for her and invited her to sit down. Very well-mannered indeed.

"I am five and twenty," Sarah said, a slight nervousness in her tone at the admission. This issue, she knew, could be a sticking point and could undo the whole interview before it could truly began.

"A meteoric rise to the top of your field, I should say," the man praised as he took a seat opposite her.

"I strive to be my best in all I undertake," Sarah said. It was both a truth and a good line she had learned to use in interviews down the years.

"And where exactly do your ambitions look to take you, Miss Price?" Mr Morgan asked, leaning into the plush leather of his chair and watching her intently. "From what I understand from my friend, you have left behind you a series of broken-hearted shopkeepers, housekeepers, and other employers who were all dismayed that they could not keep you. I wonder, Miss Price, am I just another steppingstone on your ever-determined march to greater things? Impressed though I am by your references, and while I am in no way opposed to ambition, I will confess I am looking for someone who would be loyal to the post I offer. I would not care to go through the business of hiring you and helping you become acquainted with the house and my habits only to have to replace you within a year. Now, tell me, Miss Price, If I were to offer you the position here, would I have your assurances that you would not look to advance yourself higher?"

Sarah took a moment to consider the man's words. It was tempting to throw her lot in with the handsome and supposedly generous Mr Morgan without hesitation, but prudence kept her from rushing straight into a promise that might bind her.

"You seem to be deliberating very hard over so simple a question, Miss Price. Care to confess to having your eye on a place at a lord's estate after you are done with me?" Mr Morgan still smiled, a suggestion of teasing as he pressed her for an answer.

"I am just very careful with the promises I make, sir," Sarah answered, trying to remain diplomatic. "I have been very happy in all the positions I have taken over the years, but never felt I had found my true place. "Perhaps I am guilty of having lofty ambitions, but I have never hidden that from anyone. With each new position I take on, I am quite happy to entertain the notion that I might be taking on the position that I will keep for the rest of my days, but I should not wish to speculate on the future. I have heard great things about you as an employer, but it does not follow that I should automatically enjoy working under you."

"I see," Mr Morgan said, his smirk becoming slightly more enigmatic as he considered her answer.

"I do not mean that as an offence, sir. I am thus far most impressed with all I have seen... Of your home, I mean. Still, I think it would be prudent not to become tied to a promise to remain here before I have even had time to learn your habits and your specific needs."

Mr Morgan sucked in a breath, his chest swelling beneath his black suit jacket. He nodded slowly, twice. "A fine answer, Miss Price," he complimented. "I must confess it took me pleasantly by surprise. Most times when I interview someone I find people eager to swear all sorts of promises from the outset just for the chance to get the job."

"My uncle is a bookkeeper and taught me to maintain a healthy pessimism."

"Hmm, perhaps I should look to hire him to my staff as well," Mr Morgan said as he leaned back in his chair. "Your uncle is a great influence in your life, I take it?"

"He was my guardian while growing up," Sarah answered.

"I see." For the first time since the meeting began, Mr Morgan's smile waned a little as he found himself treading into potentially unhappy memories. To Sarah's relief, he did not continue to question her about her past any further. As she had risen through the ranks and gained a name for herself, she found her unfortunate origins a hamper to her career. She did not look to purposefully lie about her childhood, but she tried to avoid speaking of it wherever she could.

For a moment, the pair sat in silence, Sarah finding that embarrassed glow returning to her cheeks as the man opposite continued to study her. Mr Morgan was not shy in his glances. He did not exactly stare at her, as some employers had in the past—no, his gaze was subtly different, almost complimentary. It might have been wishful thinking on her part, especially when she considered how attractive a man he was, but Sarah almost believed Mr Morgan had taken a fancy to her.

"My friend, your employer, is most loath to lose you, Miss Price. Considering your thoughtful and reasonable desire to test the waters of this position before making firm promises for the future, perhaps I might suggest a compromise."

"I am open to any suggestions you might have," Sarah assured with a smile that was perhaps a little too eager as she found herself becoming easier in the man's company.

"Let us see how a month goes here. You may take the time to decide if you can tolerate the way I file my papers and leave my books in haphazard piles on the dining table, and I, in turn, can decide if you make my tea too hot or weak for my palette. If, at the end of that time, you feel you could be happy working for me, I would like to ask you again if you believe you could work for me in a more longterm, perhaps even indefinite, capacity."

Sarah's own smile grew a little wider and she bit on her bottom lip as she tried to mask her pleasure. Though no employer to date had been quite so serious about gaining assurances regarding her staying on, it was nice to find herself so wanted. Mr Morgan seemed eager to keep her and, from what little impression she had gained of the man thus far, she felt like she would likely be quite happy to remain in the employ of the personable and charismatic businessman.

"I believe that is a sensible suggestion. But what exactly is to come of me if I decide the position is not right for me? Not that I believe that will be a likely eventuality," she added, shyly.

"If such a disappointing outcome were to arise, I would ask my friend to return you to his home and the post you will be leaving behind. Seeing as how he has intimated most strongly how loath he is to lose you; I believe he will be more than happy to leave your position in his household open for one month in the hope that you might return to him. I dare say he would even try and find a way to drive a wedge between us to ensure such an outcome."

Sarah laughed, catching herself as she feared she was becoming too easy in the man's company. Their conversation had only carried on a few minutes, but already they were making jokes together and conversing as easily as friends. It was not necessarily a bad thing, but it was not at all what she was used to or prepared for. Certainly, in her years of working in domestic service she had never once felt such an instant rapport and connection with an employer. That Mr Morgan was attractive to boot made the opportunity before her both more thrilling and more dangerous all at once. Sarah had heard more than her fair share of cautionary tales of servants who grew too attached to their masters. While Mr Morgan's reputation as an honest and upright man preceded him, that did not mean that she should not be cautious.

"Well then, Miss Price, should we have a drink to celebrate our new accord?" Mr Morgan proposed.

"Perhaps, I could make you that cup of tea? You never know, you may find it below your standards and wish to withdraw your offer before you are forced to endure a whole month of them." Despite her own mental checks, Sarah was still trading friendly barbs with the man, unable, it seemed, to help herself.

Mr Morgan rose from his seat, and Sarah was surprised when he quickly moved around to take her hand as she rose to join him. "If you are so keen to get to work, perhaps we can begin with a tour of my home. We can start in the kitchens, to test your skill at brewing tea leaves. Depending on your success, I shall either show you the rest of the house, or else escort you to the door."

"I never thought the shape of my entire career would ever be defined by a single pot of tea, but I welcome the challenge," Sarah said as she let herself be led through the house. It hardly escaped her notice that Mr Morgan kept her on his arm the entire time, just like lovers taking a stroll in the park.

CHAPTER 5

Sarah found herself charmed and pleased by Mr Ralph Morgan. The man was everything she had heard and better. His house was elegant without being garish, and cultured without being pretentious. In many ways, the house was an extension of Mr Morgan's own character, and Sarah was delighted to learn that the man was responsible for most of the design and aesthetic of the house: having it renovated to his own likes shortly after having bought it. Mr Morgan was rightly proud of all he had created and accomplished in his lifetime and he seemed exceptionally keen to show Sarah everything. The tour of Mr Morgan's home saw the pair well into the evening. Always, they found themselves falling into discussion and debate. Sarah was keen to hear Mr Morgan's story of how he had become so successful and diverse a businessman and how he came about his business philosophy that was lauded for both its philanthropic leanings and its loyal, hardworking labour force.

As Mr Morgan would have it, kindness and compassion had as much to do with good business as with good manners. The horse could be better led with sugar than driven with the cane. While Sarah felt the man was simply generous by nature, she could certainly understand how Mr Morgan's business strategy encouraged his workers to go above and beyond for him and how competition for any position in his factories or stores were so hotly fought over.

The only concern that crossed Sarah's mind as she bid the man adieu that evening was when she considered how little of their day's conversation had revolved around her new role in his home. As she played back all the conversations that had taken place in the various rooms of the house, the realisation dawned on her that she had asked none of the appropriate questions nor been told any of the specifics of her posting that would help her get ahead when she moved into the servants' quarters the next day.

Even this faux-pax wasn't enough to spoil her good mood, though, as she walked home. There was an extra spring in Sarah's step as she walked. She felt a little lighter and held herself a little taller as she moved effortlessly through the evening crowds with a smile on her lips that drew several curious looks from passers-by. As she considered the issue of her duties, she assured herself that Mr Morgan would laugh about it with her in the morning and give her a proper orientation to her specific duties in his home at that time. Her smile grew even larger as she imagined making him his first cup of tea and anxiously waiting to see if it met with his 'very high standards.' Yes, working for Mr Morgan had all the makings of a most successful venture for Sarah. And, despite her note of caution in the interview, her conversation with him had made her reasonably certain that she would not wish to advance herself again. If every day working under the man was to be as charming as her interview, Sarah could not think of anything more she could ask for.

As she moved in the direction of home, Sarah came to a cross street and paused. She chewed on her bottom lip for a moment as she looked to the leftward path that led across the river and away from her uncle's home. She had thought to visit with him first and share the news of her promising new position but wondered if she should perhaps stray out to the streets of her youth, and visit with her brothers. It had been some time since she had last called on them and it was very likely she would not have the time in the future, once her work as Mr Morgan's housekeeper began in earnest. Her brothers would be more pleased for her than her uncle. Though Uncle Timpson was perfectly happy to congratulate Sarah on all her accomplishments, his praise always felt distant, disinterested even—as if he was some colleague or work associate rather than true family.

Changing her course, Sarah moved down the narrower street, checking that her valuables were secured deep within her pockets as she ventured into the world of her youth.

London, as Sarah had discovered throughout her rise in status, was a world of two halves. A gossamer curtain seemed to shield one half of the city from the other, keeping the rich and powerful away from those whose circumstances offended their more cultivated senses. As Sarah pushed out across the river and in the direction of the factories and docks, the quality of travellers on the road visibly diminished, as did the quality of the houses and indeed the road itself. Though only a servant, Sarah turned heads as she moved through the increasingly claustrophobic streets. She was prim, proper, and clean amongst a sea of dirty, slovenly dressed and sweaty individuals. Some eyed her with curiosity, some with envy, others with tired, vacant eyes. A few more sinister individuals looked at her with hunger, and more than once Sarah's instincts warned her she was being followed. Years of living in these same dangerous streets gave her an advantage against those who would seek to do her harm. Most of the chancers who followed her quickly drifted away when she turned and fixed them with a challenging look, letting them know she was fully aware of their lurking in the crowds. She knew her way through the winding maze of streets and always kept to the roads and alleyways that would see her protected by other travellers. Those pickpockets who persisted on following her for any length of time were left disappointed by the lack of opportunity she gave them to make a swipe for her purse or person.

Only when Sarah came to a side street between two houses did she put herself in any risk or danger. The narrow passage she slipped down was dark and empty, not really a street at all. It led off the open path and into a small tucked-away annex where poorer families lived in conditions more squalid and intolerable than even she had known in her childhood. This was home to her brothers, three grown men for whom fortune and chance had not been kind.

Sarah's fine, black shoes were dirtied by the muddy path underfoot. She splintered her hands on the worn, worm-eaten stairwell that led to a small alcove space three floors up in the tightly packed tenement building, and no matter how well she tried to hold her nose, the stench of sewage was strong in the air. Sarah felt a familiar pang of guilt as she moved to her brothers' door and gave her familiar knock—three raps, a pause, and one final rap. She wrapped her arms about herself and inspected the squalor all around her, feeling more than a little self-conscious as a bedraggled and tired woman in a red dress and too much makeup cast her a curious glance from down below.

What would Mother say if she were to learn that this was how her boys were living now? Sarah asked herself the question so many times when she visited with them and felt a pang of guilt well up inside of her as she imagined the stern lecture her mother would have for her. She just knew her mother would blame her if she could. Her brothers certainly did. While Walter, Robert and Henry were usually civil and pleasing company, there had been two or three occasions where they had let their true feelings about their older sister out of the closet. When drunk and moody, any of her brothers would complain about Sarah's fortune and the lack of help she gave them. It did not matter to them that Sarah had no place of her own where they could live, or that her finer clothes were usually given to her by her employers. It didn't even matter much to them that she was always giving them what money she could whenever something went wrong for them—an all too common occurrence. Still, they were her brothers, and, as her mother had told her shortly before her death; one day she might have to rely on them, just as they had relied on her.

It took a while for anyone to answer the door and Sarah wondered privately just how it could take her brothers so long to admit her when their home was so small. Finally, Robert came to the door, opening it only a fraction at first, then throwing the door wide open once he caught sight of his sister.

"Sarah! And here I thought the West End had swallowed you whole and claimed you forever."

Sarah smiled at her second youngest brother, trying to ignore the grime on his face and the chip in the lower front tooth he had earned in a brawl a year back. Though she knew Robert as a caring brother, protective, and a surprisingly good listener when he was in the mood, he had grown to have a somewhat frightful appearance. Were he a complete stranger to her, Sarah often thought she would suspect him to be some sort of thug or criminal. He was stocky, with broad shoulders and muscular arms. His hands were large, like bear's paws, and his thick knucklebones always seemed to be bruised as if he had been caught in a scrap—which was exactly how his tooth had been nicked in the first place.

Robert wrapped Sarah up into an exuberant hug, lifting her off the floor and causing her to squeal as she thumped him. "Hey, put me down! We're way too old for you to be picking me up and carrying me around!"

Robert laughed and did as he was told. Sarah was quick to brush at her dress and apron, keen to check that he had not left any grubby marks on her clothes that she would need to expunge later. As she busied herself, Robert's attention drifted down to the woman in the red dress lingering in the alley.

"Hey, Catherine, busy night ahead of you?"

"Why, you hoping to sneak in a little visit my way?" the woman called up. Despite her flirtatious tone, her face looked thoroughly bored as she ran a rehearsed line.

Robert laughed again and motioned for Sarah to follow him inside. Sarah tried to put the awful woman outside from her mind, not caring to think that any of her brothers might stoop to visiting such a woman of the night.

Inside the small ramshackle building, Walter and Henry were sitting on their beds. Sarah looked over to the little stove in the corner, noting that there was no food upon it. The boys never seemed to cook for themselves, always eating at the public houses and running up additional costs on their already meagre living. That unused stove was probably the cleanest thing in their grubby little dwelling and Sarah bit her lip as she considered something.

"Do you want me to cook anything for you all?" she asked brightly.

"Ha, you're exactly like Mother." Robert laughed as he moved past Sarah and brought out a chair for her, near to the small fire.

"When you're here, maybe," Henry added, his words already carrying a barbed tone.

"I do try and come by as often as I can, but my work leaves me with very few opportunities to just come out and visit," Sarah reminded.

"Well, maybe you shouldn't have gone chasing those fancy jobs, wiping the arses of the fancy lords and ladies, and kept to honest labour," Henry countered. Sarah tried to overlook his disgusting summary of her job. She did not even bother to engage him with debate or try to reason with him. Henry had long believed that Sarah was far overreaching herself, that she should have stayed on at one of the shops where she first found work and moved out of Uncle Timpson's home to come and live with them and to help support the family.

Though it had never been expressly stated, Sarah suspected Henry was in some ways a little jealous of her. As the oldest boy, he was the one meant to be leading the family. While Mother had loved all her boys, there was something special about Henry. He was the leader and it was always expected that he should be the one his siblings listened to. He had always had Walter's and Robert's unswerving loyalty, and Sarah suspected Henry did not trust the extra freedom and individuality she enjoyed.

If Robert had the blessing of muscle amongst his brothers, Henry was still the brains. While it was being more than generous to call him smart, he had developed a smooth and confident aura about him that allowed him to navigate most situations and he was often the key to himself and his brothers finding new work. He was a smooth talker, able to read people and quickly establish how he could best win them around to his way of thinking. A slim man of wiry strength and thin, narrow features, he was, Sarah supposed, fairly good looking. Certainly, he was the only one among her brothers who went courting and Sarah had oftentimes felt a twinge of discomfort at how Henry never seemed to have the same girl on his arm for long.

Sitting down by the fire, Sarah smiled at Robert as he went over to a cupboard by his bedside and pulled out a bottle of wine. "Think we should splash out a little since we have such prestigious company?"

"You're really going to waste that bottle now?" Walter asked, the youngest brother sitting up a little and frowning at his sibling. "Since Sarah has such fancy friends, you'd think she'd bring her own wine down here so we could all enjoy a taste of that better world of hers.

Sarah frowned and ignored Walter, as did Robert and Henry. While Robert had grown up strong and loyal and Henry sharp and charismatic, Walter had the misfortune of growing up with little personality at all. Perhaps it had something to do with his being the youngest brother—always led by Henry. Walter had never managed to find his own personality and instead grew into a kind of lesser shadow of his elder brother. Everything Henry disliked Walter hated, anything Henry liked was automatically Walter's favourite thing. Were they ever to be parted from one another, Sarah fancied that Walter would be left in a kind of fugue, adrift and uncertain about anything. It was no exaggeration to say that Walter needed Henry. He needed Henry to know how to think, what to say, and how to feel. Right now, because Henry had thrown a barb at Sarah, Walter was determined to do likewise.

"Now, then, what brings you by in the evening when you should be working?" Robert paid no mind to his brothers' apathy and took a seat opposite Sarah, pouring a far too generous volume of wine into a filthy pewter cup and handing it to her. Sarah took one polite sip and then nursed the thing in her hand.

"Well, I am pleased to say, I have some news," she began, looking to Walter and Henry to check to see if they were paying her any attention at all.

"Managed to land yourself another new job, did you?" Henry asked, taking the wind out of her sails a little.

"How could you guess that so easily?" Sarah said with a pout.

"It does kind of feel like that is the only news you ever have for us," Robert conceded with a laugh, taking a generous pull of wine straight from the bottle.

"The way you've been working yourself up the greasy pole, I'm surprised you have anywhere left to go," Henry said, his voice completely disinterested and apathetic. "What have you become now, Queen Victoria's personal dresser? Commander of Her Majesty's navy?"

"Mayor of London?" Walter chimed in, eager to be his brother's parrot and get in on the conversation.

"Actually, I have become housekeeper to Mr Ralph Morgan, himself," Sarah said, sticking out her chest proudly and looking for some recognition or surprise from her brothers. Nothing in the room changed, and still, only Robert smiled at her with his distractingly broken smile.

"Is this someone we should know?" Walter asked, looking immediately to Henry for his answers.

"Come on, you've heard of him," Robert piped up to Sarah's relief and satisfaction. "That Morgan fella is the bleeding heart everyone is always going on about. You know—his factories and businesses are like the promised land. Once you start working for Mr Morgan, you'll never have a trouble in your life again."

Sarah raised a brow, interested to hear how the man was viewed by others in the city.

"Oh, that guy... We've always steered clear of that one's work," Henry said.

"What on earth for?" Sarah asked, genuinely curious. Though she would not say it aloud, she would have thought her brothers would be clamouring to get a job under a man as understanding and sympathetic to his workers rather than the hard and merciless bosses they so often ended up under.

"Seems like one big fraud to me," Henry replied with a shrug. "All this talk of his generosity and kindness—got to be a sham. The man's got an angle somewhere."

"He merely believes that a contented worker is a happy worker," Sarah insisted.

Henry sat up, a smirk forming on his lips as he looked to Walter. "Well, look at our big sister getting so defensive all of a sudden. Is it possible the man has already pulled you under his spell, or have you been charmed by his rumoured rugged good looks?"

Walter made a disgusting face and Sarah immediately turned to the fire and concentrated hard on keeping a blush off her face.

"Anyway, trying to get a job with that one is a waste of time," Henry continued. "Any time there's a space in one of his companies the queues block up entire streets. I'm not wasting an entire day loitering around for some pompous foreman to say we're too low brow for that man's company."

"Because, of course, you three have never been caught loitering or shirking work even once in your lives," Sarah returned, sarcastically. She had meant her words in good humour, a little friendly banter after her brother's teasing, but she could see by the way Henry's face pulled into a frown that he had not taken the jibe well.

"You know what, I don't think I'm in the mood to hear about what new job you've landed thanks to your always kissing our uncle's behind." Henry rose up on his feet, Walter following suit. He grabbed his fraying, old coat and moved to the door. "Congratulations on your new job. I'll keep an eye out in the papers for when you take over for the Queen."

Sarah's eyes trained to her feet and she hung her head. "It was good seeing you both," she muttered. Despite the animosity in the air, she really meant her words.

"Maybe, now you're in with Mr Morgan, you might look to help us out a bit more," Walter suggested as he followed Henry's coattails out the door.

Both Robert and Sarah sat in silence for a time, waiting until the sound of their siblings' footsteps had receded.

"Don't worry about them," Robert said, putting a reassuring paw on Sarah's knee. "Henry's been stalking about in a mood for days; ever since we lost our place at that smoking house down by the docks.

"You lost your job... Again?" Sarah closed her eyes and pinched the bridge of her nose.

"Hey, it wasn't our fault," Robert assured. And it was never their fault. Nothing in life was their fault. If there was one constant lesson her younger brothers had committed to heart that their dear departed mother had taught them, it was that they were blameless in everything they ever undertook.

CHAPTER 6

If Sarah had one complaint as she moved into working for Mr Morgan, it was the lack of work she had to do for the man. The other domestic servants knew their roles and the house ran like clockwork. Though she relished the conversations and laughter that surrounded her days with Mr Morgan, she felt more than a little guilty to be paid for the privilege of talking with a man whose company she thoroughly enjoyed.

From the start, Sarah knew there was an attraction on her part to her handsome and charismatic employer. In the first days of her work, she feared this fascination might become a point of contention and issue for her, but she quickly began to suspect that her attraction for the man was hardly one-sided. Sarah had no real understanding as to why the powerful businessman paid her any attention, but she would not deny the fact before her eyes.

It could be seen in the hours they spent conversing in his office in the evenings, and the way Mr Morgan quickly began to seek her opinion and approval on mundane matters such as his wardrobe and style. It was demonstrated in those stolen glances Sarah noticed from time to time when she walked about the room. She found herself suppressing a pleased smile every time she felt her master's eyes drawing toward her, his mind distracted from his work and reading as she went about her tasks.

What was most thrilling about Mr Morgan's attention was that he was hardly shy with them. Despite the taboo of paying such attention to a servant, Mr Morgan made no disguise of his interest in Sarah or his desire for her company. Those times when Sarah had caught Mr Morgan glancing her way were rarely followed by a hasty retreat on the man's part. Unless he truly couldn't afford the distraction, his glances would always be followed by his calling Sarah over where, together, they would descend into another pleasing conversation. He even looked to her for advice on business, valuing her opinion despite her consistent reminders that she had no knowledge or experience of running a business.

Only one question remained—where was it all leading?

While Sarah enjoyed, even craved her master's attention, she had to wonder if it could really come to anything. Mr Morgan was a man who looked beyond the trappings of class, but was he really willing to court a woman so far beneath him? She wanted to believe so, but Sarah had her doubts.

Of only one thing was she sure: if Mr Morgan's interest in her proved to be only superficial, then her place in his home as a housekeeper would never work out. After just two weeks in each other's company, they were already too familiar for master and servant.

Tidying away a book and the morning paper from the breakfast table, Sarah tried to orientate her mind away from the pleasing and simultaneously worrisome thoughts that had distracted her so much over the last days. To keep her mind centred and grounded, Sarah tried to occupy herself with some topic or issue that did not focus on the man who was quickly taking over her thoughts.

Her brothers. Now, there was a matter Sarah knew she should be putting more of her energies toward. After discovering the three had lost yet another job, she felt that she should redouble her efforts to support them. Henry's jibes at the lack of effort she put into helping them remained with her. Even the pleasing company of Mr Morgan and the halcyon days of joy she was currently enjoying were not enough to let her completely forget the ties that bound her to her brothers.

As she moved toward Mr Morgan's office, she wondered if perhaps she should take advantage of her new association. Considering her fears for what might happen should the apparent flame between them be snuffed out, she felt a need to strike while the iron was hot. There was, in her position, a real opportunity to do something for her brothers that would change their lives for the better.

In her heart, she lifted a silent prayer to God for His favour to shine upon her. Perhaps, in His grace, a way would be opened for her kin to find gainful employment. Courage rose in her heart as she approached the door.

"Well, there is an expression I have never seen on your face before, Miss Price. I think this must be the first time I haven't seen you walk in with a smile on your lips."

Mr Morgan's words as she walked into the room brought her attention back to the present moment and her natural glow returned. That her master could detect even the slightest of changes in her mood pleased her.

"Well, there is your smile returned," Mr Morgan said as he put down his work and put his attention fully on his housekeeper. "However, if something is bothering you, I would hope you would feel able to tell me all about it. I hope you have no complaints regarding your work here?"

"No, nothing like that," Sarah assured. There were her fears regarding their growing closeness, but those could be left for another day. She tried to bring herself to ask the question on her mind but simply couldn't find the words.

Mr Morgan frowned just a little, seeming to read her mind and sense her reluctance. He sucked in a breath and rose from his seat, straightening his jacket as he moved toward her.

"As it happens... I did have something I wished to ask you, Miss Price," the man said, his dark green eyes focused on her as he came to stand before her. "I hope you will not think this an abuse of your services, but I was wondering if you might join me on Saturday night as my guest at a function."

"Your... Your guest?" Sarah could barely believe what she was hearing. Her eyes darted away from his searching gaze, and she turned away, not wishing for the man to see how flustered she had become.

"Of course, I would not dream of forcing you into such a thing. If the idea makes you in any way uncomfortable then—"

"—No, I am honestly thrilled for the opportunity, though I do wonder if you have considered the repercussions. Would the hosts not have something to say about you bringing your housekeeper to a soirée?"

"If they did, I would be sure never to accept an invitation of theirs again!" Mr Morgan laughed. "I am known throughout Town for what they call my, progressive attitude. I do not care that you are my housekeeper. I have enjoyed your company here in my home more than I have ever enjoyed the company of any of the young women who generally attend parties such as these. I have difficulty making conversation with the daughters of rivals and partners in business. There is something wholly unsettling about making conversation with a girl when you know their father has all but insisted that they approach me and try to court my interest."

"I see, so I am nothing more than an instrument of distraction for you at this party," Sarah suggested. "I am to be your shield against such advances?"

"I would prefer to call you my 'knight in shining armour,'" Mr Morgan suggested. His reversion to the traditional fairy-tale lines caused Sarah to laugh.

"Well, when you cast me so gallantly, I am sure I can't refuse. I just hope you do not expect me to attend in a suit of armour," Sarah said, feeling her courage redoubling as they returned to their teasing.

"Sadly, not. While I am always willing to buck conventions, I do not think even I could get away with bringing an armoured knight as my guest to a party. I do, however, have a most fetching gown I have commissioned for you that I hope you will find to your liking."

"A... A gown?" Sarah repeated his words, lip trembling a little as she tried to imagine such a thing. In her entire life, she had never been in the kinds of finery she had seen ladies such as Miss Lucas wear. It sent a thrill through her, one of anticipation and nervousness. "You're being too kind to me, sir," she pointed out.

"I thought you might have some qualms, hence why I ordered the gown ahead of time," Mr Morgan said with a mischievous smile. "I have arranged for you to take the afternoon off tomorrow for a fitting."

"I'm curious what you would have done had I refused your invitation," Sarah said, brushing aside a lock of her hair as she tried to keep her excitement under control.

"Either I would have kept it as a gift for you in the future or saved it for the next servant to join my household."

Sarah shook her head and sighed again. The idea that she would be attending a fancy soirée with her employer still hadn't sunk in, and she needed a moment to process things.

"I hope the promise of this party goes some way to helping you forget your troubles. Though, please, if you need my help with something, you have but to ask."

Sarah bit her bottom lip. She needed to seize her chance. "I... I have a request I would like to ask of you," she blurted out a little too fast.

"Oh yes?" Mr Morgan asked, raising a brow and leaning against the wall as he listened.

"After all your kindnesses to me, I feel I am stepping well beyond my bounds to ask you such a thing but..."

"Out with it," her Master encouraged, putting a hand on her shoulder. "If it is within my power to help you in any matter, I would be more than pleased to do so."

"I have not spoken of my family before, but I have three brothers who are currently out of work in the city," Sarah confessed.

"I had no idea," Mr Morgan said, looking somewhat surprised. "I will confess I had noticed your tendency to avoid speaking of your past and I did not wish to push the subject. But I must confess I am surprised you never mentioned having siblings."

"We have not had the closest relationship growing up. After our mother died, my uncle took us in. Sadly, he never formed a good opinion of my brothers, and their opportunities in work were severely limited as a result."

"Yet, your uncle helped you advance to where you are today?"

Sarah pursed her lips, unsure of how she should respond. She did not wish to be drawn into too deep a conversation, lest she say something that might go against her.

For the first time since she had entered Mr Morgan's house, an awkward silence passed between them.

"...I would be happy to assist your family in any way that I can, Miss Price," Mr Morgan assured. "If you would like to invite your brothers here to—"

"—No! No, I couldn't possibly do that." Sarah shook her head. "Just the possibility of meeting with one of your foremen at any of your businesses would be a great boon and opportunity for them." Sarah watched as her master's eyes narrowed. She knew well enough that she was being evasive and prayed he would not push the matter.

"Very well, Miss Price," Mr Morgan replied. Something in his voice had changed. Sarah could not quite explain what was different, but she felt a sudden shift in her master's manner. His smile remained and he did not appear at all uneasy. All the same, the way he turned and moved back to his desk felt different to her. He seemed a little tense in his movements, no final teasing word or apology before he returned to his work.

"Should I leave you to your work, Sir?" Sarah asked, adopting a more formal air.

"I should return to work, yes. I shall draft a letter of introduction for your brothers to one of my trusted foremen. You may take the letter to them when you go out to have your dress fitted, ahead of the party on Saturday."

Sarah should have felt thrilled and elated at her success in giving her brothers the opportunity they needed. Still, as she left the room, she felt oddly nervous, and worried in a way that left her feeling nauseous. She had to give her brothers the benefit of the doubt, but she feared what might happen if they squandered the opportunity she was forging for them.

The day of Sarah's dressfitting brought mixed emotions for her. She found her mind flitting between feelings of excitement, wonder, anticipation, dread, fear and guilt all at once and often threaded together. Mr Morgan's generosity and attentions continued to bring a smile to her face but, somehow, Sarah felt worse for having brought up the matter of her brothers with him. Mr Morgan had already done so much for her in the few weeks she had known him, and now she had the gall to ask more of him. What was worse was the fact that she couldn't bring herself to tell the man about her brothers.

Things had changed subtly in the house since that meeting. The walls Sarah had put up around her family and her past had the unwanted effect of putting a barrier between herself and Mr Morgan. It came as a sign that she did not fully trust him and he responded to that distrust by withdrawing. This was not to say he ignored her or treated her with indifference. In manners and kindness, Sarah found her master to be the same as always. However, he seemed to ask her fewer questions and showed more reserve in his conversation. Sarah could not tell if he was doing so out of a desire to respect her privacy or whether he was, in fact, purposefully holding a part of himself back from her.

Still, Sarah had reason to be proud. If she put aside her selfish feelings and girlish fantasies of finding love with her employer, she could be satisfied in having given her brothers the opportunity they so sorely needed to rise out of the vile neighbourhood where they spent their days. Sarah consoled herself with the sure and certain knowledge that their mother would have been proud of her for having put her siblings before her own happiness. She was sure that putting the boys in Mr Morgan's path would be good for them. As he was an understanding and tolerant man, she hoped her brothers would have a chance to thrive without being immediately thrown out on their ears. She liked to imagine that the fairer conditions under Mr Morgan's employment might also have the added benefit of making her brothers more conscientious workers as well. While Sarah liked to believe that her brothers really were the victims of bad luck when it came to working, she knew they were ill inclined to fight for jobs they thought were beneath them.

∼

Her fears and wishes died away when Sarah arrived at the tailor's for her fitting. For one glorious hour, she was transported to heaven as she was given a tantalising taste of the dress Mr Morgan had selected for her. It was a dress of dark green, almost the very same colour Sarah had remembered Miss Lucas wearing in Mr Edwards's offices all those years ago. It billowed out near the bottom, the black lace at the hem dragging just a little on the floor as she walked. Sarah enjoyed swaying her hips, studying the way the dress moved with her—almost like watching lush grasses swaying in a summer breeze. And the fabric of the gown... Its texture was so delightful to the touch that Sarah feared she'd never be able to keep her hands off of it. She adored the way the fabric moved between her fingers, the cool crisp texture of it as she ran her palm over the dress to smooth it out. She was sure she looked quite shameless pawing over the gown as she was, and Sarah put effort into maintaining her composure as the tailor's assistant inspected her and noted down the necessary adjustments that needed to be made to the sleeves and waist. Being waited on in such a manner was a thrill all of its own and Sarah couldn't help but wonder if this was a taste of what was to come if things continued between her and Mr Morgan as they had been.

The opulent fantasy of the dressfitting seemed to flit by all too fast, and Sarah soon found herself treading down the familiar pathways in the direction of her brothers' home. The spring in her step was gone and she found herself moving with deliberate slowness as she tried to decide on the best way to tell her brothers about the opportunity which she had cultivated for them. The biggest obstacle would be Henry. Henry was proud and stubborn. Caught in a pinch, he'd happily come to Sarah for money. But, when it came to less tangential forms of support, her eldest brother was always lukewarm at best.

Slipping into the grim and shadowy back alleys, Sarah hastened her pace as she made the last turns and climbed the rickety old stairwell to her brothers' door. She gave the usual knock, surprised when no one immediately answered her. There was a light clearly visible from under the doorframe so she knew at least one of her brothers had to be home. She pursed her lips and knocked a little harder, determined not to make a wasted trip. She then pressed her ear to the door, convinced she could hear voices whispering from within.

Then, all at once, the door opened and Sarah almost fell into Robert. Her brother looked down at her with a frown, casting a look back inside and then choosing to step out and close the door behind him.

"What's with all these unexpected visits, Sarah?" he hissed. Sarah was surprised to see her brother so tense. As he looked back at the closed door behind them, she was certain she saw something like fear in his eyes.

'Is this a bad time?" Sarah asked, peering to the door curiously.

"We just... have some company round... Discussing a delicate matter... A proposal really."

Sarah's eyes narrowed. The way Robert stalled between his words, it was all too obvious that something was afoot and it couldn't possibly be a good thing. When her brothers kept secrets from her it never turned out to be anything positive.

"Who's in there," Sarah asked, her voice becoming low and challenging.

"Just Jimmy and a few friends," Robert said, eyes nervously averting from Sarah's as he spoke.

"Jimmy? Just what are you three doing still running around with that good-for-nothing crook. He's been nothing but trouble for you ever since the bakery incident."

Sarah's hackles were raised. After everything she had done, the imposition she had made asking her employer to give her brothers a chance, she was not going to hear of them associating with Jimmy again. That man was a bad penny, always turning up just when her brothers ran into another rough patch. Sarah didn't know how Jim did it. She swore he must have spies always keeping an eye out for whenever Henry lost another job.

"So what scheme is that layabout trying to rope you into this time?" Sarah asked, cutting straight to the heart of things. She knew full well Jim never visited her brothers unless they could do something for him. That was just the kind of fair-weather-friend he was.

"Jim's just visiting," Robert repeated, sticking to official lines.

"Well, then, it won't be too much of a bother for you if I were to come in," Sarah countered. She had her brother cornered. Robert could only own up to the truth or else let her come inside. Sarah was quite certain that her brothers would not breathe a word of their real discussion with Jim to her, but at least her presence might keep them from agreeing to anything dangerous or rash. Several times already Jim had tempted her brothers to skirt the bounds of the law. To Sarah's relief, they had never been caught, and their crimes were really little more than misdemeanours. Still, if she did not keep a careful eye on their dealings with Jim, there was always the chance their little misadventures could take a more sinister turn.

Robert, at last, opened the door, letting Sarah in. Henry sat by the fire with Jim in the guest's chair. Both were leant forward, their pensive faces suggesting it was anything but a social call. Walter stood behind his older brother like some faithful hound at his master's feet, and all three turned and gave questioning, slightly irritated glances Sarah's way as she intruded upon their meeting, whatever it was.

"Miss Price; you're looking well," Jim cooed. Despite being made of bile and venom, the boy had a smooth tongue and always laid on the compliments thick and fast. Sarah suspected Henry's own charismatic ways were learned or borrowed from watching the older boy down the years and copying his moves.

"Jim, it's been a while. I don't think I've seen you around here since... Since the last time my brothers lost their jobs in fact," Sarah returned. Her barb did nothing. Jim continued to smile at her serenely, her jibe not even making the habitual sinner flinch.

"Perhaps if you visited your brothers a little more frequently then you'd know I still check up on my boys often enough. At least I come calling when my friends need me, not when I feel like rubbing my success in their faces."

Sarah didn't want to show weakness, but she couldn't help but frown. Jim had a good read on her and picked his line of attack well. It was true her visits often accompanied some good news from her life. Perhaps, she truly was riling her brothers up the wrong way by always coming round with stories of her success? She had hoped such stories would motivate them, that they would at least be happy for her. But as she considered Jim's words she wondered if she was perhaps deluding herself.

"Why have you come over, anyway?" Henry asked, cutting between the pair and looking to Sarah impatiently.

"You haven't left that Morgan job and become a lady in waiting to the Queen, have you?" Walter asked, recycling the tired joke from her last visit and impressing no one with it.

"Morgan?" Walter's words seemed to strike a chord with Jim and Sarah swore the man's eyes seemed to sparkle as he looked at her with renewed interest. "You've landed yourself a job with Ralph Morgan? Mr Perfect Employer and saint of the city?"

"Landed a position as his housekeeper, wouldn't you believe," Henry said.

"Well, that really is news," Jim said, leaning back in his chair and continuing to stare at Sarah with a look that troubled her greatly. The way he eyed her at that moment, it was the same way a fox would stare down an injured pigeon. Sarah tried to pay the man no mind and instead looked at Henry.

"It's because of Mr Morgan that I am here, actually," she said, digging into the pockets of her dress and pulling out the letter of introduction her master had written up for her.

"What is this?" Henry asked seeming quite reluctant to take the thing from her, as though the envelope might be poisoned.

"It's a letter," Sarah said simply. "I spoke to Mr Morgan and mentioned the trouble you've had finding stable work. I asked if he might have a vacancy in any of his businesses and he was kind enough to pass on this letter of introduction. You can use it to meet with one of his stewards at his textile factory. It isn't far from here. If you work hard, the three of you together would have enough money in a month to move out of this place and rent a decent apartment in the city.

"And I bet we'd have even more if you were just willing to share a little of your earnings with us. I bet you make more in a single day than the three of us would make in a week and you have board and lodging on top of that."

"I am just doing what I can to help you," Sarah replied, lowering her gaze and heaving a sigh. Of course, Henry would have to find fault with the opportunity she'd created for him. Then, to her surprise, aid came from a most unlikely source.

"Now, come on, Henry," Jim began reaching over and taking the letter from her brother. "Seems to me like your sister's really sticking her neck out for you here and a job at Mr Morgan's is not the kind of opportunity you pass up. I would love to get me, or one of my boys, a cosy position in one of his factories or shops. The doors it would open..."

Something in the way Jim spoke that last line set Sarah on edge. With Jim, there was always a darker underline to every word that spilt forth from his filthy mouth and it concerned her to find him so keen on encouraging Henry to take a second look at the letter she had given him. She looked to her eldest brother, studying the way he and Jim exchanged looks. The pair really were closer than she would have liked and seemed to almost be communicating in the silence, their conspiratorial glances suggesting some hidden conversation beyond the one in the room.

"Well, I suppose I can have a look at this," Henry said, placing the letter in the inner pocket of his jacket and patting it to make sure it was safe and secure. "If that's all you wanted, Sarah, then I hope you don't mind me cutting short the visit? Jim and I really do have a lot of catching up to do and—"

"—No, no," Jim said, rising from his seat with that easy smile still on his lips. "I was merely coming by to check that you three troublemakers were getting by, but I can see your sister has things well in hand. We can meet again another time."

Sarah studied Jim carefully as the man moved past her toward the door. Something in his words had set her on edge. Then again, the man's very presence set her on edge.

"You be sure not to waste the opportunity your sister's given you. You three don't know how lucky you are. I'll come by again soon, hopefully, to celebrate your new job."

Sarah's brow furrowed as she watched Jim leave, wishing she could decipher what was going on in that head of his. She knew he did not have her brothers' best interests at heart, but hoped his plans were benign. If she was lucky, Jim's desire to push Henry and her other brothers toward work with Mr Morgan was just so he could scrounge money off them from time to time once they had a little more money to their name. She hoped it would be that simple.

With Jim gone, Sarah knew she wouldn't be getting any answers about his true motivations and she tried to put her fears behind her as she looked to her brothers. Henry was already eyeing the letter again, having pulled it back out from his pocket to study in detail. He seemed oddly alert and studious and it burned Sarah up to think that her brother would only countenance her generosity if one of his friends told him it was a good idea to do so.

"This letter then... Do we have a job at his factory or not?" Henry asked.

"It's not a promise of employment, no," Sarah confessed. "Mr Morgan is a cautious man and would never hire someone he doesn't know without an interview, even with a recommendation."

"Did you at least put in a good word for us?" Henry probed, eyes narrowing as he looked to his sister. Sarah didn't answer him, but the nervous way she wrung her hands together gave him his answer. "Didn't think you'd have it in you to stick your neck out that far for us," he criticised.

"Look, you are lucky to have this opportunity, and I will have you know I did stick my neck out just by asking the man to consider you for a position," Sarah snapped. "Do you think servants just get to ask their masters casually if they might consider hiring their family. I've only been in the man's home two weeks and made a real imposition in asking him for this."

Henry said nothing, just pursed his lips and stared into space as the gears in his mind turned slowly. "If we're going to make good on this opportunity, we'd best know what to say to the man we're going to meet. You know this Morgan character. What do we need to say to make sure we get a look in for this job?"

Sarah took a seat opposite her brother. She was still not comfortable with his attitude to the offered work, still nervous about Jim's interest in their opportunity.

CHAPTER 7

The days leading up to the soirée with Mr Morgan's friends was drawing ever closer, and Sarah felt herself drifting further apart from her employer in similar degrees. She told herself she was not wrong to push the man into considering her brothers for employment in his businesses. Still, as hard as she tried to reason away her actions and justify herself, Sarah felt a growing feeling inside her that she had betrayed the man. Try as she might to deny it, she knew that Henry, Robert and Walter were not the types of men her employer would ever have considered hiring without her recommendation. She knew too that, despite the new interest her brothers had taken in the offered work, they were not loyal to Mr Morgan in the way others were, and would not feel that same gratitude that others did. Then, there was the matter of Jim and the interest he had taken in her brothers' new opportunity.

Try as she might to justify her actions and shoo away her fears, Sarah felt a rising anxiety inside of her as the days wore on. There was no specific fear, just a general unease and worry that her brothers might ruin everything for her. What made this fear all the more maddening was that she could not confide her fears in Mr Morgan.

How could she go to her employer and tell him that she had fears about her brothers working under him when she herself had pleaded their case? How could Mr Morgan trust her again if she admitted to their past failings and litany of disappointed bosses they had left behind them in their short span of years?

Sarah had doomed herself to silence, a silence made worse by her employer's perceptive eyes. She knew beyond the shadow of a doubt that Mr Morgan was aware there had been a change in her. He seemed very alive to her mood and it almost disappointed her to find that he respected her privacy enough not to force her to talk to him. A part of her yearned for her employer to summon her to his office and demand that she tell all that was on her mind.

Two days before the party, Sarah was granted her half-wished-for summons, and she moved to her employer's office with trembling footsteps, her mind running wild with a thousand scenarios of what Mr Morgan might say to her.

Mr Morgan had mentioned a desire to speak with her at breakfast that morning. There was no emotion is voice, nothing to hint at disapproval, but his deadpan expression was worrisome all by itself. More importantly, the fact that Mr Morgan felt a need to schedule a meeting, rather than just speaking his mind at the breakfast table suggested a certain formality to the proceedings, further evidence of his hardening heart and the growing distance that had come between them in the last days.

Coming to her master's door, Sarah noticed that it was closed; a new and unsettling sight. She straightened her back and knocked lightly. She hoped Mr Morgan would laugh at her formality and tell her not to worry so much. But all she heard from the other side of the door was a professional, 'Enter.'

Sarah opened the door and slipped inside, finding her master sitting at his desk with several papers before him. He seemed to be in the middle of composing a letter and he took a moment's pause to finish his train of thought on the page before looking up at Sarah. It would never have been that way a week ago. A week ago, Sarah was quite sure the man would have gladly thrown down his pen and abandoned his work the moment she entered the room.

"Please, take a seat," her master invited. The politeness was as before, so was a smile, but everything felt so professional now.

"You wished to see me, Sir," Sarah enquired. She could feel her heart palpitating fast inside her chest. It was only two days before the soirée. Could Mr Morgan have come to regret inviting her to the party and now looked to rescind that invitation in light of their growing coldness.

"I would like to ask your opinion on a matter," her master said. That came as a surprise. It had been days since Mr Morgan had sought her advice on any matter and it was odd indeed that he should so suddenly desire it again.

"I will do my best to offer what assistance I can," Sarah said.

"Your brothers... How would you describe them? I am looking for your personal take as the one who knows them longest and best."

Sarah tensed in her seat, her fingers gripping the armrests as though she might be suddenly thrown to the floor. She took a deep breath and tried to think of an answer that was both honest and diplomatic. She could guess well enough that something must have happened for Mr Morgan to be asking the question in so serious a voice.

"I take it from your silence you are having some difficulty forming an answer to the question?' Despite Mr Morgan's combative words, Sarah felt no malice or ill intent from him. If anything, he sounded disappointed.

"I just... I do not know what to say about them," Sarah said, trying to buy herself a moment. Why had she not rehearsed an answer for this? She had spent so much time imagining being interrogated by her master on this very question and yet she had not taken the time to formulate a suitable answer.

"Would you call your brothers trustworthy?" Mr Morgan asked, narrowing the focus of his question as he continued to study her. Those eyes that Sarah had once been so thrilled to feel gazing towards her now sent a shudder through her.

"I... I must ask... Has something happened?" Sarah could not find her words and she hated herself for it. Her loyalty to her siblings prevented her from answering Mr Morgan and her loyalty to Mr Morgan prevented her from lying to him also.

"You seem very fast to suspect something," Mr Morgan observed. He took a deep breath, eyes moving away to gaze upon the fire. It was as though he could not stand to look at her at that moment. Sarah said nothing, waiting for her employer to explain all that had happened.

"I will admit, it would be so much easier if your brothers had been caught doing something," her employer mused. "As it happens, my workers reported the three young men before anything could happen, alerting me to suspicions that concern me greatly."

"Suspicions?" Sarah felt her mind calm a little, relieved that her brothers had done nothing concrete to jeopardize their employment. At the same time, she felt a stirring of frustration.

"I have been told the three of them behave very differently to others in my employment. They keep to themselves, often lingering after work and finding their way to places in my factory where they have no business being."

"They could have merely been wanting to get to know the place," Sarah suggested. "You would hardly have blamed me for wandering the rooms of your house in the evening to better learn my way around the place. More than once you have caught me browsing the bookshelves in your library."

"…That is true," her employer said. "Still, their movements have alarmed my foremen and others in my staff, people I trust implicitly. They have mentioned your brothers lingering near doors. No one can get a good look because one of them will invariably be acting as a lookout while the other two are obscured round a corner. My men tell me freely that no one has seen anything, but they have heard things and suspect your brothers may be looking to work out which doors to the factory are weakest…"

Sarah felt bile growing in her as she readied herself to defend her brothers once again, just as her mother would have wanted, just as she was sick of doing after so many years. She sucked in a breath, eyes narrowing as she looked to fight for their corner.

"Honestly, Mr Morgan, I am a little disappointed that you would look immediately to judge my brothers. You have always seemed the type who would not be blinded by prejudices and others' presuppositions."

"I have only the word of my other employees to go on," the man said, frowning a little as he found himself at loggerheads with her. "You should know I take great care in selecting my employees, and each has proven themselves trustworthy. When they come to me with suspicions of this nature, I cannot simply ignore them."

"Well, I say maybe you should," Sarah replied. "I have seen this pattern of behaviour in relation to my brothers and I am sick of it. Just because my brothers live in a poorer community, because their clothes are a little worse for wear and Robert is so intimidating to look upon, they always end up cast as untrustworthy."

"I can sympathise with your frustrations, Miss Price, but your words do lead to further questions in and of themselves."

"Such as?" Sarah's reply was snappy, combative. Of all people, she had not expected Mr Morgan to be so doubtful and judgemental with her brothers.

"Such as the previous employment record of your brothers before you asked me to extend them an offer of work," Mr Morgan said. "My foremen were diligent enough to come to me with more than just suspicions and factory floor gossip. After the workers expressed their fears and concerns regarding your brothers, my men decided to dig a little into their previous employment history."

"I see... And you found therein a series of disgruntled employers who never gave them the proper chance they deserved. I will have you know my brothers have never once been arrested or charged with committing a felony in their place of work."

"No, it is true that my men uncovered nothing to suggest that your brothers are criminals... but, Sarah, really: fired for laziness, sleeping during work hours, arriving late, brawls with other workers. Even if I put aside the more alarming suspicions my foremen have brought to me, I am surprised by what they have uncovered about your brothers. I am... if I am truly honest, disappointed that you did not have the decency to tell me of their past difficulties."

"I am not going to apologise for what they have suffered in life, the opportunities they were denied. Can you really say you would have welcomed them to your factory if I had mentioned their employment record to date?"

"I would have hoped you'd have given me the chance to surprise you on that score, at least," Mr Morgan said. "You have been open and honest with me since the day you arrived here. We have... or I had hoped, at least... formed a real connection during your time here, one based on our mutual respect and trust in one another. Ever since that day you recommended your brothers to me, you have been acting out of character and out of sorts and I may say that you knew that this reckoning was coming."

"So, now you judge me?" Sarah's nostrils flared and her lips drew thin. "Do you wish me to leave your service—are you to dismiss me as well, now that you know my low connections?"

"I am not looking to dismiss you, Miss Price. Though, if you wish to leave my service?"

"And my brothers, what of them?"

"In light of what you have revealed and what my foremen have learned, I have decided to dismiss them," Mr Morgan said, his voice grim. "I know they are your brothers and your loyalty toward them is admirable. Still, it sounds to me like your brothers expect you to haul them out of any hole they dig for themselves, and you excuse them for no better reason than because they are family. You went out of your way to recommend them to me and they jeopardised not only their own career but your own through their actions."

"If your foremen's suspicions were to prove real and not some over-excited imagining…" Sarah replied. She still could not believe what she was hearing and she stood up, not able to stay in Mr Morgan's presence any longer.

"Are you leaving?" the man asked. The question was open-ended but Sarah knew what he was truly asking. She looked back at him. Despite her anger, Sarah's care and regard for her employer would not permit her to storm out of the house in a rage.

"I... I need time to process this... Please, may I be excused?" she asked, remembering her place as a housekeeper.

"Take what time you need," Mr Morgan replied, offering a sad smile. Sarah turned on her heel and left.

CHAPTER 8

Sarah walked at a pace, hands clenched and lips pursed thin as she moved through the streets to find her brothers. Her errand was, in fact, to pick up the gown she was due to wear to the soirée at Mr Morgan's friend's, but she had resolved to meet with her brothers afterward to encourage them.

Picking up the dress Mr Morgan had ordered for her seemed like a wasted effort after her confrontation with him the night before. While Mr Morgan hadn't specifically withdrawn his invitation to the party, Sarah felt sure it would come soon. Picking up the gown from the shop was now nothing more than a formality. The tailors must have sensed something was amiss when Sarah came to collect the dress. She could not summon the will to feign interest in the gown or pretend to be excited. She even refused to try it on, assuring the tailor that it would fit just fine. The tailors did not fight her on it, sensing perhaps that she was in no mood to be trifled with.

Sarah clutched her new gown, folded and wrapped in an ornate box underarm as she marched to her brothers' home. She did not care how others looked at her on the way. She did not bother to ward off the opportunistic pickpockets and thieves who shot her fascinated glances. If any tried to swipe the expensive dress from under her arm she'd gladly let it go. She did not want the thing anymore and having it stolen would mean she would no longer have to worry about the soirée. Still, no chancers made to take the large box from her. Perhaps they thought such a prize was too rich for them to get away with.

Coming to the small side path that led to the back-alley den where her brothers resided, Sarah noticed a group of people stood out on the stairs leading to her brothers' small apartment. Even from a distance, Sarah knew these were Jimmy's crew and their presence suggested something was seriously wrong. She sucked in a breath and quickened her pace down the alley.

Sarah quietly cursed her employer and his cavalier decision to suspend her brothers. The three had suffered enough at the hands of distrustful employers and Sarah could only imagine where they might go from here. With each new rejection and dismissal, her brothers were being pushed closer and closer to the life of crime Jimmy led. She had no doubt their 'friend' was there hoping to recruit them, persuade them to give up on the straight and narrow and tread a darker path. Determined not to let her siblings give up, Sarah pushed past Jimmy's boys on the stairs and fought her way to the front door where Henry seemed to be in the middle of a tense conversation with his so-called 'friend.'

"Look, how was I supposed to know it would end up like this?" her eldest brother said, his voice a whining hiss. As Sarah slowed up and looked between her brother and his visitor she wondered if Jimmy really was trying to tempt Henry to darker work as she had suspected. Jimmy's expression was one of anger and impatience. His usual rogue's smile was absent, and his arms were crossed tight across his chest as he listened to Henry. Behind him, a rough-looking man, tougher even than Robert, lurked like some trained attack dog.

"Hey, boss, the boys' sister is here," one of the other men said, alerting Jimmy and Henry to Sarah's presence.

"Well, well... And I guess we have you to thank for this?" Jimmy sneered. "I tell you, Henry, I bet your sister was the one who landed you in this mess. Probably ran her mouth to Morgan from day one about your troubles."

Sarah knew what Jim was doing—divide and conquer, set her brothers against her so he could win their loyalty for himself. She looked to Henry, dismayed to see how easily her brother fell for Jim's tricks. He was staring daggers at her, his eyes moving to the box in her hand as he sucked in a breath between gritted teeth.

"What are you here for this time? To show off your income by flaunting your purchases at us?"

"That is a very expensive looking box," Jim said, seeming to notice it at the same time. He had a possessive look in his eyes and Sarah screamed as one of his boys grabbed the thing from behind her.

"Hey, don't you dare touch that!" Sarah cried uselessly as the ruffian behind her threw off the ribbon and opened the box.

"Well, isn't this pretty," the man said, grabbing the dress by the collar and pulling it out to show the other boys. Sarah looked to Henry for support, but her brother just looked away as though pretending he hadn't noticed or seen anything. Something was wrong. Jim never took these kinds of liberties with her. Ever.

"You know, I am not one for fashion, but I think this dress could probably fetch a pretty penny. I don't think I'd be able to hawk it for all of the debt... But I could see my way to writing off half and giving you boys a few more weeks to put together the rest."

"What are you talking about? Debt?" Sarah asked, looking to Henry.

"Why, didn't Henry tell you? After getting the job with Mr Morgan, Henry and your brothers wanted to live large as kings and I was willing to give them a substantial loan with expectations they would repay me in kind."

"Just how much is this loan we are talking about?" Sarah asked, frustrated to find her brothers living so carelessly, yet again.

"Eighty pounds," Jim said flatly.

Sarah's eyes widened as she looked to her brother, hoping against hope he would say it was all some elaborate jest.

"Just how do you even have eighty pounds to lend away?" Sarah asked incredulously. "That's more than you could ever hope to earn in a year."

"I'm certain a fine upstanding girl like you would rather not know how I get my money," Jim returned.

"Well, eighty pounds is a lot, you can't have spent much of it," she said to Henry. "Give Jim back what you have, and I can cover the rest with my own wages."

"I lost it already," Henry said.

"What... How?"

"None of your business," Henry snapped. Sarah flinched. Her brother hated being made a fool at the best of times and she should have known he would not admit to his folly now.

"Our boy got a little cocky, betting down by the docks, and your brothers were very keen to live large the days after they got that job.

"Sarah, can you just give Jim that dress of yours?" Henry said. His lips were pursed together and his cheeks pulled in as if he were being forced to swallow a bitter fruit asking her for aid.

Despite her earlier desire for some thief to come and steal the gown from her, Sarah was loath to give it up to Jim, of all people. She looked to her brother and then to Jim, and finally to the gown that was her gift from Mr Morgan.

"It's... It's not mine to give," she was surprised to find herself saying. "My employer ordered it as a gift." Sarah didn't dare say it was a gift for her.

Jim looked to his men, his confidence wavering a little as he looked to the gown.

"Don't think for a moment I can return to my employer and tell him I simply lost a dress that valuable," Sarah added.

"Fine, but you better find some way to get that eighty pounds to me by Sunday next," Jim warned her brother. "If I don't have what I am owed, then you better believe I will find some other way of extracting what you owe me."

Sarah's eyes widened, alarmed at the obvious threat. She knew Jim was no friend of her brothers, knew he was a villain, but she had never heard him threaten her brothers this way before.

"Come on boys, let's leave Henry here to talk things out with his sister. I'm sure, he wouldn't want to suffer the indignity of begging her to bail him out of trouble... Again."

Henry shot Sarah another hateful glance, and she could not for the world think why. Was he truly going to blame her for hurting his male pride? Fortunately, he was not so proud as to send her away. As Jim and his men began to stalk away down the steps to the alley, Henry nodded for her to step inside his little rundown apartment.

As soon as Sarah was inside and the door closed behind her, she looked to her brothers. Both Walter and Robert were sitting on their beds, Robert looking shamefaced and downcast and Walter just looking to Henry for cues, as always.

"What on earth!" Sarah screamed, flying into an aggressive rage she had never known in all her years looking out for her brothers. "Why would you think to borrow eighty pounds from Jim just when I have found you a perfectly respectable job in Mr Morgan's factory at better pay than you had ever known?"

"Hey, don't you start shouting at us. Your precious and oh-so-good employer kicked us out on our ear within days," Henry returned with his own barb. "How were we to know. You told us he was a sure thing."

Sarah sighed, running a hand over her creased forehead as she tried to calm herself. "Yes, I will admit it was unfair of Mr Morgan to suspend you based on fearful rumours from his staff. It galls me to the core that you three always face such prejudice, but still... Eighty pounds? Even if all had been well with the job and you had settled into the roles without trouble, that is an absurd sum to borrow."

"It wasn't really a loan," Robert corrected, causing Sarah to frown.

"Shut your mouth, Robert," Henry barked, casting a nervous tell-tale glance Sarah's way.

"No, you tell me right this minute, Robert, because I have spent all of yesterday fighting with Mr Morgan to get you your jobs back and even threatened to leave his service if he does not treat you fairly. So, if anything is going on here that I need to know about then you tell me now or I will not help you pay even a single pound back to Jim, do you hear me!"

"Sarah, come on, you wouldn't. We're family," Walter whined, looking at her with expectant eyes and a smile that suggested he expected her to simply cave in to their whims. That look riled her, reminding her of Mr Morgan's observations the previous day that she had tried so hard to refute.

It sounds to me like your brothers expect you to haul them out of any hole they dig for themselves, and you excuse them for no better reason than because they are family."

"No, you know what... I am deadly serious," Sarah said, earning a surprised look from Walter who looked immediately to Henry for support.

"Didn't you hear Jim? They're going to get men after us if we don't pay up? You can't really just let them do that to us?" Henry said. "What would Mother say?"

"Just what makes him think he can threaten you at all?" Sarah asked. "I have never seen Jim act like that, ever. This must be about more than money. Tell me everything that's going on here… And I want the truth!"

"Come on Sarah, you don't want to know what we need to do to scrape by when the whole world is against us," Robert moaned. "We get told we're not pulling enough weight in a job and before you know it, we're out on our ear. We had to do something to get by in those lean times."

Sarah felt an icy chill run down her back. She did not want to ask what her brothers had resorted to in order to get by, but as she considered the reports Mr Morgan's men had made, a fearful suspicion settled in.

"You couldn't… Don't tell me you fell into the same dodgy work Jim is always offering. I thought you were better than that!"

"Maybe we wouldn't have had to if you just looked after us as mother had always asked," Walter interjected.

"You know well enough I gave you all I could to help you survive," Sarah returned, in no mood now to be made the villain or scapegoat. "It's you… It's you three living large and never saving a penny, always shirking off and blaming your employers for not understanding you. I've… I've defended you three for so long, but I just can't keep pretending anymore, not when you try and blame me for your misfortunes. It is your fault you are in this mess. I mean, really, what kind of idiot would think to borrow eighty-pounds and then spend it all in two weeks!"

"I am not an idiot!" Henry roared. He rushed forward, eyes wide and body trembling with anger. In all her years, Sarah had never seen him like this. Then again, she had never stood up to him like this. He was in her face, spittle hitting her cheek as he roared at her. Robert stood up, uneasy.

"We had a sure thing with Jim! That eighty-pounds was our payment for letting his boys sneak into that dumb factory and help themselves to a few bits and pieces to sell from time to time!"

"What?" Sarah's face turned white and she felt ill inside as she stared in disbelief at her brother. "How could you!"

"Oh, come on, Sarah, don't go defending that employer of yours. It wasn't like we were going to steal his life savings. He makes more than enough not to notice a few odd bits of merchandise going missing from time to time!"

"You three really were trying to test the doors and find ways out of the factory, weren't you!"

"Maybe we wouldn't have tried our luck if you hadn't sold your man as a bleeding heart and a soft touch."

"I never called him either of those things," Sarah admonished. "I told you he was a good man who cared for his employees and treated them fairly."

Henry snarled at her, turning his back on Sarah as he stalked to the far side of the room. "You can think what you like about us. I think it's pretty clear our uncle changed you. You're not a Price girl. Mother would turn in her grave if she saw you picking Mr Morgan's side over your own brothers."

Sarah sucked in a breath, lips pursing as she felt a steely resolve settle over her. "I never said I wouldn't help you, Henry," she replied.

Her words earned a surprised glance from Robert and that irritating grin from Walter. Henry turned more slowly, his anger melting to reveal the charismatic, placid smile he usually reserved for his women. "I'm sorry I shouted at you. I should have known you still knew your place... Deep down. And I promise you this will be the last time we will need you to bail us out. Now, tell me, do you have eighty pounds you can lend us to sort the debt with Jim?"

"No," Sarah said. She noticed Walter fix her with a doubtful expression and repeated herself again. "No! I do not have eighty pounds just lying about. What kind of money do you think I make to have that kind of sum just ready to hand to you?"

"Easy, Sarah, let's keep our voices down," Henry eased, still keeping to his calmer voice. "I can think of one way we can get what we need, but you need to promise that you are with us. I need to know that you understand that we are just doing what we need to do to get by."

"What were you thinking?" Sarah asked, her voice resolute and firm as she looked at her brother.

"That dress you have, it's for a party, right? Does this mean Mr Morgan will be out of the house someday soon? Perhaps taking some lucky lady out on the town."

"Actually, he had invited me to the soirée with some business associates."

"Even better," Henry said with a smile. "All you need to do is one thing for us and we will be able to give Jim what he wants, avoid a beating, and settle the score with that Morgan for throwing us out in the first place. And you don't have to worry, we'll make sure nothing leads back to you, Sarah. All you need to do is go to that party and leave us a way into the man's property."

"I know just the way in," Sarah said. "I guess... I guess I have no choice and, as you say, it would never have come to this if Mr Morgan and all those others had just treated you fair. I guess it's time I stopped pretending."

Henry smiled, pulling Sarah into a rare hug as he kissed her forehead. "That's my girl."

CHAPTER 9

Sarah stood in her bedroom, inspecting herself in front of the full-length mirror. Her gown fitted her beautifully, hugging her upper body like a glove and accentuating her figure. The corset beneath was not done up too tight and Sarah felt quite comfortable in the dress. Her hair had been made into an elegant braided updo; the braids held in place by pins adorned with beautiful diamonds. The way they sparkled in her hair; it was as if crystallised raindrops had settled on her head. Gold earrings and a matching necklace, inlaid with emeralds, completed the look and left Sarah feeling like a duchess, every bit as refined as Miss Lucas, and more. To dress in such finery should have left her heart soaring. But Sarah could only frown as she looked herself over in the mirror.

"You look truly beautiful," a voice from behind her caused Sarah to turn and she looked at Mr Morgan for a moment. His face, too, was grim, not at all celebratory or content as he stood before her in his finest. Sarah tried to hold his gaze, but her gaze moved to the floor as she hung her head and heaved a sigh. "We should probably go down to the carriage soon."

"It is already waiting for us," Mr Morgan said. He tried to smile again, but it didn't hold. With a stiff motion, the man put out his arm and Sarah took it dutifully as she let him lead her downstairs to the door.

At the bottom, Sarah left Mr Morgan's side, moving to the back of the house to put out the lights and, more crucially, to ensure the servants' door was left unlocked. When she returned, her face was stony and resolute, looking far more like she was set to attend a funeral than a party. Mr Morgan said nothing, linking his arm with hers as they stepped out into the night together.

∽

"We can go, they're in the carriage," Walter whispered to his brothers. The youngest of the trio had been put on watch duty, lingering in the shadows of the alley as a lookout, while Robert and Henry lingered in the darkened backstreets of the row of houses. Walter rushed back to his brothers, frowning as he noticed Henry wasn't moving. "Come on, I said they're in the carriage?"

"Yeah, I want the carriage to move before we go sneaking inside," Henry explained in an exasperated voice. "What if that Morgan fella has forgotten his pocket watch."

"Let's hope he has, all the better for us," Walter said, licking his lips in anticipation.

"Remember, we need to make this look like a proper break-in," Henry said, going over the plan again. "Once we're inside we need to turn the place upside down, and Robert, you need to smash up the back window and door... Make it look like we forced our way in. But make sure you keep the noise down as you work."

"Don't worry, I know how to break things quietly," Robert assured. "I'll just scuff up the door a bit and it'll convince the bobbies that someone went at it with a crowbar.

"Good." Henry nodded, taking several deep breaths as they waited for the sound of hooves to signal their sister's and Mr Morgan's departure.

"I must say, I didn't think Sarah would go along with this," Robert mused. "I never thought she'd understand what we need to do to get by."

"Don't fool yourself into thinking Sarah is happy with any of this. She is definitely looking down on us, just like always. But she knows that family is everything and she wouldnt want to disappoint Mother. Don't think she'll do this for us again, and we best never let her think we're ever going to do something like this again. She'll probably make us promise, after we're done here, that we're going to go down the straight and narrow, living in poverty and honesty instead, rather than living as we should."

Henry fell silent, head cocked to the side as he focused on the sounds around him again. "Sounds like they've gone," Henry said at last. "Let's get moving."

Walter began to dart down the lane, Henry grabbing him by the collar before he could get too far.

"Let's not rush and make a commotion. They're going to a party, after all, and we don't need to rush ourselves breaking in."

Together, the three brothers moved down the dark street to find the back entrance of Mr Morgan's property. Henry put out a hand to the wooden door, pushing it open and sighing in relief as he felt the door give, letting him inside.

"Thank god..." he breathed. "Right, Sarah's given us our way in. Now, let's sort out what we need for Jim and maybe grab a little extra for ourselves. Whatever you do, let's not make too much noise until we're ready to leave."

∼

Moving through the small back garden of the property, Henry felt his confidence rise as he opened the next door into the kitchens. He would not admit it, but a lot was riding on Sarah behaving herself and doing as she was told. Her outburst after learning of their arrangement had almost been her undoing. In that moment of anger, Henry could have sworn she was a different person. She was, in a startling way, more the girl Henry remembered from his youth, not the facsimile of their mother who always seemed to understand how hard things truly were for them and helped them without question or reserve. Henry had thought that more spirited side of Sarah had died along with their mother, but this latest escapade let him know he should be on his guard for the future. As it turned out, Sarah did still have some limits on what she would accept her brothers doing, and those limits were nearly reached.

Stepping into the kitchen, Henry reached in the dark, feeling his way to the counter where he was pleased to find a candle and matches waiting for him. Sarah had been very good to think of that touch and Henry wondered what other uses she might have for him and his brothers if only they could convince her to lose some of her scruples.

Lighting up the match, Henry looked around, eyes narrowing in the dark as he took in the kitchen. Of course, there would be precious little in the back worth looking at and he only took a minute just to inspect the room and take in the layout before moving on to the next door.

"Robert, you start working on that door, make this look like a proper break-in," Henry ordered as he moved forward with Walter ever his faithful shadow. He moved confidently to the door, stepping out into the hall and smiling as he took in the more opulent decorations—the soft carpet underfoot and paintings hanging from the wall.

"Best treasures will be in Morgan's office and bedroom," Henry said. "You take the stairs and check his room, I'll find his office."

"Whatever you say," Walter replied, moving casually past his brother to the stairs, an excited grin on his face.

"Don't get anything too heavy or conspicuous, all right?" Henry reminded him as he watched his brother pass by. "Remember, once we're out of the house we still need to get everything back home without being stopped by anyone."

"I've got it," Walter insisted, sounding just a little insulted as he made his way up the stairs. Henry turned his attention back to the bottom floor, looking to the doors around him and trying to decide which led to the master's office. Thoughts of the treasures held within left him excited for the days ahead, his imagination firing with thoughts of how surprised Jim would be when he came to him with enough treasures to wipe their debt and leaving the pickpocket owing them money.

Henry had just moved to the right-hand door and put his hand to the silver handle when he heard something from upstairs. He rolled his eyes and heaved a sigh as he guessed Walter had tripped in the dark without a candle of his own to light his way.

"Take your time, Walt; we've got hours to work this place," he called.

"Henry! Henry, run, it's—" Walter's voice called out panicked and loud. Henry froze in place, eyes wide as he looked to the top of the stairs. The worst suspicion took over him and his hand on the door handle withdrew. He began to move back, trying to control his breathing as he kept an eye on the stairs.

"Henry! Henry!"

Henry turned, pulse racing as he heard Robert shouting now from behind, leaving him in no doubt as to the danger he was in. He put all thoughts of his brothers and the house behind him, running straight toward the front door, looking for an escape. Robert and Walter were done for. Henry didn't know or care what or who had come for them. All he cared about—all he needed—was to get out.

Reaching the front door, Henry slammed against the wood and rattled the handle desperately. He pulled as hard as he could, swearing as he tried to coax the door open. When that didn't work, Henry took a step back and kicked the door as hard as he could with his boot. Nothing helped and he finally turned to see what was coming for him. Down the stairs charged two men in the distinctive uniforms of the law. Bobbies.

Henry gave up. There was no getting out and he was not going to risk his hide fighting the officers of the law. With a deep sigh and a hateful look on his face, he put up his hands in surrender as the two men charged into him, turning Henry full about and pressing him into the door as they put him into a painful armlock.

"Argh! Easy, I'll cooperate. I'll cooperate."

The policeman did not seem to pay Henry any mind, adding more pressure to his grip as the eldest Price brother shouted his complaints in vain.

∼

Sarah bit down on her bottom lip, wringing her hands nervously as the carriage finished its turn and began the final clip down the street. She had stared out the window the entire journey, her eyes glazed over and looking blankly ahead as she waited for their wrap-around tour of the local neighbourhood to come to an end. Mr Morgan had remained quiet in kind, keeping a sombre and respectful silence as he sat by her. Only now, as they neared his home, did Sarah notice him shift in his seat and look at her with concern. A hand reached over and held hers, preventing her from fidgeting any further. Sarah was startled by the sudden, intimate touch but did not look to discourage it.

"Do you think they have them?" Sarah asked, not even sure what answer she wanted to hear.

"I would be very surprised and lose a lot of faith in our constabulary if they were not able to capture three thieves in so easy a trap," Mr Morgan mused. He did not sound happy or smug in his answer and his brow was creased with concern as he continued to study Sarah. "You know, Miss Price; I owe you an apology."

"An apology? When I am the one whose brothers planned to rob you in your factory and in your home."

"I really do owe you an apology," Mr Morgan said again, squeezing her hand in his a little tighter. "When I confronted you the other day… when I accused you of being your brothers' pawn… that was clearly wrong of me."

"No, it wasn't wrong," Sarah said, her voice matter of fact. "Truth be told, I needed to hear that. I needed to have someone point out to me how blind I had become to my brothers' true nature, how much I overlooked because they are 'family.'"

"At the least then, let me tell you how much I admire you," Mr Morgan continued. The carriage had come to a halt, but he did not look to get out immediately. "I can't imagine how hard it must have been to act against your brothers like this."

"I only did as I always promised Mother I would," Sarah replied. "I acted in their best interests. Only, your words showed me that what was right for them, sadly, was not what they would wish for."

Mr Morgan nodded and took a deep breath as his driver opened the door for them.

"You might wish to remain in the carriage, Miss Price," her master suggested.

Sarah smiled but shook her head. "I know you have my best interests at heart, but I think I need to face this. It would not do to hide from my brothers in this."

"Very well, I will be with you all the while," her master assured.

~

Coming to the front door, Mr Morgan rapped three times, waiting for the officers inside to let him in. The lights in the hall were all lit now and the bobbies brought to his home now congregated around the dining room where Henry, Robert and Walter could be heard running through a myriad of pleas, excuses, and threats to those who had captured them. Sarah lingered in the hall for a minute, clinging tight to Mr Morgan's arm as she listened to the pathetic sound of her brothers. She felt a fresh surge of guilt threaten to overwhelm her as she considered how much she was to blame for how this had turned out—how her inaction and decisions had led them to this pitiable point.

Mr Morgan remained by Sarah's side, a silent and constant companion. He did not rush her into the dining room, giving her the moment she needed to compose herself as she tried to work out just what she would say to her brothers. She knew they would not understand, she knew they would never forgive her. Still, she had to try.

Entering the room, Sarah tried to walk tall, to keep her eyes on her brothers and not to look away or hide as she let them see her. This was important. She needed the three of them: Henry, Robert and Walter—especially Henry—to see that she was not ashamed of what she had done. She did not want them to believe that this decision would become a regret for her. She would not let them form the mistaken belief that they were somehow the victims here, that she was in the wrong and knew herself to be so.

"Don't you look fancy," Henry said, his voice thick with bile as he looked Sarah up and down. "Are these the rewards for betraying your own family?"

"Do not speak," Mr Morgan said, his voice low and commanding. At his words the bobbies guarding the three brothers leaned in closer, letting the boys know that they were more than willing to enforce Mr Morgan's orders with force if given the excuse. Sarah watched, focusing on keeping her lip from trembling as she watched Henry grow silent.

"I want you three to know that I never wanted this to happen to us," Sarah began. She eyed each brother in their turn. "You may think I am here to punish you, maybe to mock you for having trapped you here as I did. But, in truth, I am here to apologise. When Mother died, I looked to honour the one promise she made me swear to before her death. I promised I would always do all I could to look out for you. For years, I thought that meant acting as Mother would have, defending you at every turn and always taking your side in any and every situation. Now, I realise I should have looked to the example of our uncle. He may not have loved any of us, as mother had, but he understood the need for you to learn that the world does not revolve around you—that you are responsible for your choices and actions. If I had realised this sooner, maybe I could have prevented you from coming this far down a path that will only end in ruin for you."

"You don't call this ruin?" Henry returned. An officer stalked forward to strike him, but Sarah put out a hand, a sign that he should hold back.

"You brought yourselves to a point where you were willing to break the law, steal from the most respectable of men, people who would have helped you and been the making of you if you'd let them and not tried to exploit them. If I had not brought you here today, if I had not put an end to this, you would only have gone down a darker path in trying to pay back Jim. What I have done here… your punishment… it will be severe, but it will, I pray, be better for you than the paths you were forging for yourselves. Those trails would only have led to Jim killing you or pressing you further into a life of crime to pay him back… I dread to think how much he was already talked you into down the years."

Mr Morgan patted Sarah's arm as he too looked to the boys, adding his own voice to her censure. "Your sister has done you a great favour by forewarning me of your plans to rob me. Had you entered my home and taken my possessions, I would have hounded you till there was no safe place for you in the city. You may think yourselves clever, but it would not have taken much for me to guess at who might have been bold enough to rob me. And when I caught you, I would have looked to punish you to the full extent of the law."

"But you are not though, right?" Walter asked, looking between Sarah and her master. There were actual tears in his eyes as he choked through his words. "You can't… it's not our fault. It was Jim. Jim was the one who pushed us into this… We didn't have a choice."

"Shut your mouth," Henry hissed.

"No, Henry," Walter replied, refusing his brother for the first time in his life. "Look, whatever we can do, we'll do it. We can work something out, right? And then you'll let us go?"

Sarah took a deep breath. "There will be punishments for all three of you. Prison, and likely some form of labour for what you have done. It grieves me to think of it, but it is what you deserve, and maybe even what you need. But Mr Morgan has assured me that he will not look to pursue the worst of punishments for you. You won't find yourselves sentenced to hanging for what you tried to do here."

"And, if you can be of assistance in bringing this 'Jim' to justice, I believe that would curry favour with the courts."

"I can tell you where Jim lives… We know where he likes to keep his stash and… and his haunts."

Walter was singing like a bird. Henry just looked off, sullen and angry, to the wall. Robert was quiet but looked more genuflective than the other two. While he was not running his mouth trying to save himself, Sarah couldn't help but wonder if something had gotten through to him. The way he looked down at his feet, the way he couldn't meet her eye or Mr Morgan's… could it be genuine remorse?

"Please, save your confessions for later," Sarah said. "I am sorry it has come to this, truly I am. I want you to know though that, when all this is done, I will still be your sister and I will still be there for you in whatever capacity I can."

"You're not my sister," Henry returned. "You're nothing… You're just a greedy, selfish—"

The bobby Sarah had restrained before moved in and smacked Henry before he could utter any profanity. Sarah gasped and took a step back.

"I think it is time we let these three go— to let them consider their actions alone," Mr Morgan suggested.

Sarah nodded, turning around and walking out of the room before she lost her composure. She was determined, till the last, not to let her brothers see anything they could misconstrue as weakness or guilt on her face. She knew they would not understand that the tears that threatened to spill from her cheeks weren't those of guilt for what she had done, but tears for what she had not done through countless times and opportunities past.

CHAPTER 10

Sarah sat in the living room chair. It was not her right. Mr Morgan had not invited her to sit down, nor was she on any kind of a break that would excuse her for her actions. She was meant to be dusting down the living room but had been stopped in her tracks when she had seen the paper on the small coffee table, opened to an article that could not fail to catch her attention.

'Family of incompetents to be deported.'

'Foiled thieves make an embarrassment in court as their sentence is issued.'

Sarah had stared at the article for what felt like an age, unable to tear her eyes from it and unable to continue her work until she had read it in full. She had not even truly noticed what she was doing as she moved to her master's chair and studied the article closely.

The journalist responsible for the piece looked to make light of the whole affair, and Sarah could well imagine readers of it would smirk and laugh at the stupidity of her brothers. Much was made of the way the trio were lured into a trap by brave and intelligent officers of the law, working with the fine and upstanding Mr Morgan. Sarah's name was not mentioned at all in the article, something she was most grateful for. The article continued to tell of how the brothers had helped bring justice to another villain—Jim Peterson. As Sarah read the article, she could tell the journalist was less than impressed with the brothers for giving up all they knew, bemoaning that there was no honour among thieves.

Sarah read through the whole thing, never stopping or putting the paper down, even when the writer's joking and mocking account of her brothers set her blood close to boiling. She had to read through to the end to know just what had happened to them—what punishment had been laid down for their crimes. When she reached the end of the article, Sarah felt her breath catch and her body stiffen as she read the words.

Prison and hard labour.

Sarah continued to gaze blankly at the paper in her hands long after she had finished reading. Her breathing had become heavier and she fought to keep control of her emotions at that moment. She was to be left alone. Though she knew from the start that labour away from London was the likely punishment her brothers could look to receive for their crimes, it was another thing to see it written in print. Her brothers were to be shipped away and there was no telling if they would ever return to her. The ties that bound her to her brothers were as good as broken and, in their severance, she found herself left alone.

A knock at the door reminded her that she was not as alone as she had supposed.

"Miss Price?" Mr Morgan stood in the doorway, uncertain and patient.

Sarah immediately threw the paper back onto the side table and leapt out of her chair as if the cushions were filled with hot coals.

"Mr Morgan, please forgive me. I should never have presumed to sit in your chair. I should have been… I mean I was just getting ready to—"

"—It is quite all right," her employer said, moving into the room. Sarah watched as he stepped boldly toward her, taking her hands in his as he looked to her with concern and care that left her feeling reassured. "I should not have left the paper there, and open, for you to discover. After I read that article, I took some time in my office to consider how I would break the news to you. I should have thought that you might catch sight of it."

"You do not need to reproach yourself," Sarah assured. "In all honesty, it was probably best that I read the article alone and absorbed the news quietly.

"Even so, I wish you had read of it from a more sympathetic source. The writer seemed to make light of the whole story in a way I did not approve of."

"It is what it is," Sarah said with a shrug, her head hung low as she let out another sigh.

"How are you feeling?" Mr Morgan asked.

"I have certainly felt better," Sarah admitted. "It is strange to think that I am now alone in the world. They… Well.. for all the harm and heartache they have given me over the years, they were my brothers."

"I more than understand," Mr Morgan said, rubbing his thumb and forefinger gently over the back of Sarah's hand as he looked to her. "I want you to know though, no matter what fears you may have to the contrary, you could have family here still, if you so desired."

"You think I should try to forge deeper bonds with my uncle?" Sarah said, giving a wan smile as she shook her head. "For all his kindness to me growing up, he never really cared for me. His main motivation was always to raise me to a place where I could pay him back for all he had done for me."

"It was not your uncle I was referring to, Miss Price," her employer corrected, causing her to look at him with confusion.

"Then, what are you suggesting?" she asked, feeling a slight tingle of anticipation inside of her as she recognised that familiar look in the man's eyes, in his smile. It was the same as she had remembered when first she had begun working for him. It was that old, intriguing gaze that suggested regard beyond that any a master should have for their servant. After all that had occurred with her brothers—with her own deception—Sarah had not thought to see that look on her employer's face ever again.

"When you first entered my home, I found myself immediately drawn to you, Miss Price. As I have watched you, I have marvelled at your grace and poise in handling your brothers and keeping your moral compass. I have found that regard growing even more. What started as warm regard and affection has, in the shortest of times, blossomed into something far deeper… A need. I need to know that you will not leave my side. I wish to make to you a proposal that I hope will be agreeable to you, one which ensures that neither one of us is left alone again."

"Mr… Mr Morgan, what are you saying?" Sarah could hardly find the words as she watched the man before her move down onto one knee.

"I own that this is perhaps not the ideal time, in light of what you have just learned…"

"On the contrary… I… I believe it is a perfect time," Sarah encouraged, tears once more staining her vision. These tears, however, were far more welcome than those that had come before when she considered how alone she might be. She watched with heightened expectation and disbelief as her words encouraged her employer on.

"Miss Sarah Price… Would you do me the greatest honour and consent to becoming my wife."

"Yes!" Sarah spoke the words without hesitation, literally throwing herself into her employer's arms and clinging tight to him as she realised that she was not to be left alone after all. Even before the unpleasantness with her brothers, she knew Ralph Morgan to be exactly the kind of man she would wish to marry, and she could hardly believe this fondest wish could be coming true.

Kneeling on the floor together, Sarah let out a grateful and relieved sigh as she felt the man's hands run through her hair, soothing her with his touch as he held her in a reassuring embrace. Slowly, timidly, their lips met.

Still kneeling, their bodies tingling and hearts soaring, they prayed, thanking the good Lord for bringing them together, and vowing to trust Him wherever He may now lead them.

EPILOGUE

Sitting in the living room, sewing quietly, Sarah watched as her daughter and son played near the fire. It was winter. Christmas had brought an air of excitement to the house. The mantle was decorated with a row of holly, their red berries and dark green leaves adding extra festive cheer to the room alongside the wreath hung by the door. Christmas was a pleasing time for Sarah, and she enjoyed seeing her children enjoy the festivities of the season in a way she was never able to growing up. Of course, she was sure never to spoil them, always ensuring they knew that any gifts they received were dependent on their good behaviour. As a mother, she was always careful to ensure her children never grew up conceited, never grew up feeling entitled, as her brothers had been allowed to do.

For all the cheer of the season, the joys of Christmas were dampened by the lack of contact she had with her siblings.

It had been two years since her brothers had been released from jail. Sarah had tried writing to them on their release back into society, letting each of them know that she would always be there for them to support them as a sister if they wished it. When she had first sent those letters, she had feared her brothers might reply at once with the hope of moving in or begging money from their sister who had done so well for herself in marriage. Perhaps, because they knew just who she had married, or maybe out of an ongoing grudge, no such replies came.

Sarah could not say she was entirely surprised. She was disappointed, but not surprised. The way Henry, in particular, had looked at her that day he was hauled away to answer for his crimes, she knew then he would never forgive her.

A knock from the front door brought Sarah out of her reverie and she glanced toward the living room door. Ordinarily, the housekeeper would answer, but her husband was already standing by the door, having just come out of his office nearby.

Sarah sat and listened quietly, trying to discern just which of her husband's many associates and friends had come to call. She frowned as she tried to place the voice, knowing it to be familiar but unable to put a name to it.

A few minutes passed and, finally, Ralph came into the room, wearing an expression partway between surprise and uncertainty that left Sarah perplexed.

"Well, who is it?" she asked gently, noting that the front door hadn't even been closed. A chill breeze was already filling the house, and she bristled as she waited for her husband's answer.

"It is your brother, Robert," Ralph answered.

Sarah's mouth dropped open. Her children looked to her with questioning eyes and she stared back, her lips pulling into a nervous and surprised smile. But she couldn't get ahead of herself. "What... What does he want?" she asked, trying to maintain her calm.

"I believe it would be best if you ask him yourself," Ralph said. "I will be right by you."

Sarah nodded and rose from her chair, bidding her children stay where they were. Ralph waited for her to step out into the hall, closing the living room door behind him as he led his wife to the door.

"Robert!" Sarah gasped to see her brother, older and looking a little tired in the face, staring at her. He smiled, revealing that one chipped tooth.

"Sarah... I know I should have written you a letter, announced that I was coming, but..."

"No, it's all right," Sarah assured him. She wanted to run straight out and hug her brother, but she held back a moment. "What... What brings you here?"

"I wanted to thank you... To thank you for what you did for me. I know Henry and Walter would disown me for coming here... but we haven't spoken for years now, anyway. I meant to visit sooner, but I guess I was ashamed."

"Robert," Sarah smiled, a relief filling her to see her brother before her, seeming like an entirely new man. "You really forgive me for what I did to you?"

"There is nothing to forgive," Robert said with a shrug. "You were right to do what you did. If it weren't for your actions that night so many years ago, who knows what would have become of us."

Sarah looked to Ralph who smiled at her and gave an encouraging nod. She parted from her husband's side and stepped out into the cold street, immediately wrapping her arms around her brother and holding him in a tight embrace. "You don't know how much it means to me to see you again."

"I feared you wouldn't care to see my face again," Robert whispered in his sister's ear as they held one another.

"I told you back then, you will always be family," Sarah said. She pulled away sniffing a little as she smiled at her brother and then looked back to her husband.

"You know, Robert, we were going to sit down to dinner soon," Ralph said, easily picking up on his wife's desire.

"Why don't you join us. It would be a pleasure to have you join us."

"Are you… Are you certain?" Robert asked, looking nervously to the man he had once tried to rob so many years back.

"Yes, I am certain," Ralph said with a nod. "You are as much my family now as your sister is."

"I'd love you to meet my children. It would be a dream come true for them to have an uncle they could know."

"You have children?" Robert asked, eyes going wide with genuine delight and excitement.

"Come in and meet them," Ralph said, moving aside from the door to let their visitor in. Sarah, sensing her brother's reluctance and shame, led him by the hand, letting him know through her gesture that he did not have to fear anything. The ties that bound remained and could only grow stronger now he had come back to her.

∼

THANK YOU FOR CHOOSING A PUREREAD BOOK!

We hope you enjoyed the story, and as a way to thank you for choosing PureRead we'd like to send you this free book, and other fun reader rewards…

Click here for your free copy of Whitechapel Waif
PureRead.com/victorian

Thanks again for reading.
See you soon!

HAVE YOU READ?

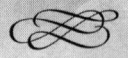

THE DESPERATE CHRISTMAS ANGEL

Have you enjoyed Sarah's story? The difficulties she faced and overcame to pull her family through were valiant.

If you love stories that ring with resilience and courage such as the one you have just read, you will definitely enjoy Eleonor Cornish's other wonderful book The Desperate Christmas Angel

It's a seasonal tale that can be read any time of year!

Eliza Thorn's straightforward life of toil and danger is about to change irrevocably, when she comes across a stranger almost swallowed in icy waters…

Here for your enjoyment is the beginning of Eliza's story.

VICTORIAN ROMANCE

The Desperate CHRISTMAS ANGEL

Eleonor Cornish

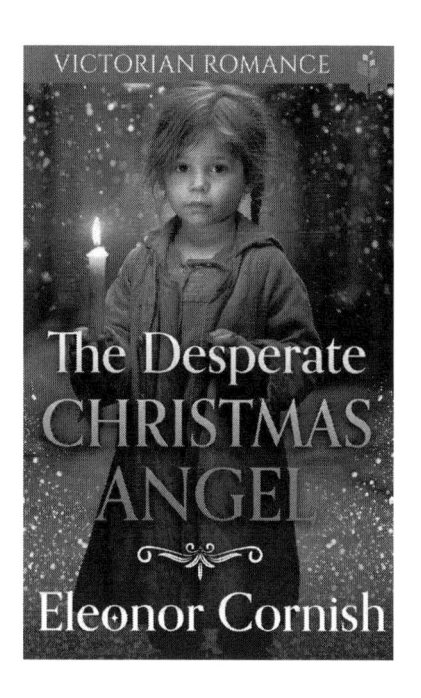

There was something very satisfying about the crunch underfoot as Eliza trudged over the frost-covered ground. She took a strange delight in finding small, frozen puddles and deliberately pressing on them with her boot. She did not know why, but she found a thrill in watching the ice shatter into tiny shards, discovering not a drop of liquid water beneath. The hardened mud was equally fascinating to the young girl, and she looked out for boot prints she had made in the last days. Seeing these preserved marks in the ground scattered alongside trails of water birds and the occasional fox gave the winter-locked moors a certain timeless quality, a sense of the eternal in a world that was so often changeable and impermanent.

As she trudged haphazardly over the frozen mud banks, Eliza took time to admire the shadows about her, the ghostly suggestion of dead logs, half sunk trees leaning heavily in the peat, the occasional shrub eking out a solitary existence on the scattered islands of dry ground that rose above the waterline. The thick morning fog was a constant on the moorland. In summer, the veil of mist was lit up in a golden sheen, bathing Eliza's world in an almost heavenly glow. In winter, the grey mists were almost impenetrable, Eliza's eyes only able to see twenty or thirty feet in any direction. Walking alone among the indistinct shadows made her feel like she was moving through some waking dream state, everything insubstantial and ethereal except for her. Some would have found the shrouded isolation of the moors depressing, melancholic, but not Eliza. She found the barely navigable and ever-changing waterways exciting, calling to her sense of adventure and discovery as she charted her way through the unmapped fog.

An expert in judging the ground beneath her, Eliza made her way across the boggy ground without once slipping into the ice filmed water or straying onto a damp patch of mud that had not yet frozen over. Eliza prided herself on how well she moved across the quagmire, claiming often that she was lighter than air to her younger brother who lacked the balance and shrewd eye to make it across the bogs.

Coming to a suitable place to begin her work, Eliza shrugged off the large satchel she carried, laying it down on the firm, frozen grasses where she stood. Then, bending down, she tested the mud around her. The slight sheen on the surface suggested the ground was still damp and she nodded approvingly as her finger sank easily into the cold muck. She withdrew her hand and wiped the dirt off on a rag she had stuffed away in her bag. Taking off her coat and laying it down by her pack, Eliza shuddered momentarily from the cold that nipped at her. She rubbed her arms and blew out a sigh, watching as the steam carried from her lips onto the frostbitten air. The cold was something she would simply have to endure for a time, and the small girl tried to reassure herself that her coat would feel all the warmer when she put it on again.

Rolling up the sleeves of her dress, Eliza once again returned to her knees, leaning as far over the damp mud as she dared without risking falling in. She bunched up her face, lips disappearing altogether as she drove her arms deep into the mud.

The liquid ooze was thick and cold. Eliza did not much care for it in any season, but winter was by far the most testing time for her. She drove her arms in up to the elbows then became still as she let herself adjust to the cold bite of the muck and stagnant water pooled around her. To help with the process, she looked up, staring into the fog and enjoying, once again, the ethereal shadows that surrounded her on all sides. She could see the curtain-like branches of an old willow somewhere ahead, the tree looking like a long-necked woman with her hair cascading down into the water. Elsewhere, a wood pigeon could be heard calling out through the gloom. Narrowing her eyes and focusing a little harder still, Eliza was sure she could see the distinctive spindle legs and noble frame of a heron trudging slowly through the mud, questing through the mire for some fish or perhaps a hibernating frog to enjoy for its breakfast.

At last, the chill bite of the muddy water subsided, and Eliza felt able to begin her work. Pulling her arms out of the water, she grabbed a jar from her satchel and then plunged it deep into the water. This time, she pushed her arms even further into the muck, trying to reach the very bottom. She scooped the thickest mud into the jar and then hauled her arms out. It was hard going. The thick mud held her fast, a horrible wet sound echoing across the wetlands as she fought the suction. At last, though, she pulled herself free and was able to pour the mud out onto the bank beside her. She spread the muck thin over the frosted grass, smiling with relief as she immediately spotted three black, blob-like entities that lay dormant and still among the ooze.

Leeches.

Opening up a second jar, Eliza deposited the three leeches inside, leaving the lid open. The tiny parasites inside did not move at all, each frozen in winter hibernation, which was exactly how Eliza liked them.

Leech picking was no job for the faint of heart. No matter the season, there was always some element of the job to be reviled and hated. In winter, it was the cold and chill of working in the icy waters that got to Eliza. However, at least in those months, the Leeches were nothing more than jewelled blobs she had to dig out of the mud where they slept. In summer, leeching was a good deal easier and a good deal more painful at once. In the warmer months, when the foul parasites were active in the waters, Eliza had to use her own body as bait to catch the little bloodsuckers. She would wade out into the shallow waters and simply wait for the leeches to become attracted to her. They would latch onto her flesh with their cruel jaws, their body's pulsating and fattening as they sucked her blood. She would pull each one off her body and deposit them in a jar just as she was doing now, but the act of pulling the lock-jawed creatures from her flesh was always painful. Even after years at the work, Eliza still felt a sharp sting every time one of the bloodsuckers attached themselves to her and every time she pried them off her.

Shuddering as a stiff breeze whipped through the willows and across her back, Eliza tried to remember the pains of hunting for leeches in the summer, reassuring herself that she was better off frozen and bite-free than warm and riddled with marks all down her legs.

∽

The morning's work was favourable for Eliza. As the sun rose and the mists that surrounded the waters eased, she felt quite confident she would be finished with her grim duty before afternoon. Mr Barrows, the village doctor, would be impressed with her time and the number of leeches she had collected over the morning—three jars full. Buoyed by her success, Eliza allowed herself a moment of repose, pulling her arms out of the mud and resting on the banks for a few minutes. Common sense told her she would be better off finishing her work. The sooner she topped off her last jar with leeches for the doctor, the sooner she could be home and warming by the fire. Still, Eliza wanted the break, and she enjoyed the views of the still, quiet moorland that stretched out before her. At least, the moors were almost still.

Somewhere farther away in the thinning mists, Eliza spied a figure moving through the mud. She could not make out any details, just a shadow, arms spread wide and stance constantly shifting. No doubt, whoever the explorer of the bogs was, they were unused to moving over the shifting mud. The heron that had spent the morning prowling the waters took to the air, angered by the interruption the blustering interloper was causing. Eliza frowned, watching the shadow closer as it seemed to struggle to find its way. She knew almost all the fishermen, fellow leech collectors and ramblers who wandered the fenlands, and none of them would have so hard a time navigating the mud. She could only assume, whoever was ahead of her was new to the task and she could not help but worry.

Twice in quick succession, the shadow seemed to dip, a poorly placed foot sinking into the mud and threatening to send the shadow falling into the mire. Each time, the shadow righted itself, but Eliza's fears were growing moment by moment. There were not many accidents or deaths recorded out on the fens, but they were not unheard of either. Almost always they involved some drunkard or a bold fool who had ventured out across the swamp without fully appreciating the dangers and challenges the wetlands posed.

Eliza's body was tense, and she knew she could not return to her work while some idiot was blustering about and at risk of harming themselves. Forgetting the possibility of an early finish and the fire of home, Eliza resolved to leave her pack and jars and go to the stranger's aid. However, just as she stood and looked to ensure her things were secure, a cry caused her to look up with fearful eyes. The shadow was gone, disappeared beneath the waters.

∽

Young Edward Stanford had stormed off onto the fens without much preparation or forethought. Impetuous by nature, governed by his heart rather than his head, he could have done little less when his elder brother had dared him to venture out across the wetlands and bring back a toad as proof of his success.

Edward was in a long and protracted war with his brother —at least he saw it that way. Martin was always crowing about his rank and seniority as the elder brother, always eager to remind his little brother how his fortunes would rise and fall on his say so. In Martin's mind, Edward was little more than a glorified servant of the household, someone to boss about and order as he saw fit. If Edward objected, Martin would remind his little brother of his place and recite again all he could do in adulthood to make his life a misery.

Of course, Edward did not stand easily for his brother's jibes and threats. Though young, he was not to be intimidated by those older or bigger than him. It had led to more than a few tousles between the lads, Edward inevitably leaving the fight with a bruise or black eye. When their mother had intervened and finally warned Martin to watch his manners around his younger brother, Martin had found a new way to keep his irksome pest of a sibling at bay…. dares.

Whenever Martin did not wish to be bothered by Edward or felt a need to punish his younger brother for some misdeed or other, Martin would invent some new dare and 'test of courage' for Edward to overcome to prove himself a man. In the last six months, he had his little brother climbing the tallest tree on the estate and stranding himself in its upper boughs, spending the night in the hayloft of the stables and bringing their mother into a frightened panic when it seemed her youngest had run away from home, and even had Edward steal their father's gold-plated pen from his office. That last hiding had earned Edward a severe rap across the knuckles and Mr Stanford had all but denied his existence for a good fortnight afterward.

Now, Edward had been convinced to embark on another quest to prove himself: to venture out into the frozen, winter-locked waters of the mudflats and find a hibernating toad. Once again, Edward had fallen for his brother's mischief and, once again, put himself in greater danger than he had first realised.

"Wow, this bog is wetter than I thought. Mother is going to kill me when she sees the state of my boots... I'll have to wash them in the servants' entryway and claim the dogs dragged them out in the snow..." Edward spoke to no one in particular as he trudged over the narrow patches of dry ground before him. The winter's cold nipped at him fiercely, his feet particularly feeling the effects after having been submerged up to the knees thrice already since he had started his journey. Mumbling incoherently to himself helped steel his courage, helped him to ignore the trials of the wetlands and keep himself centered on the task before him.

It was only now, deep into the boggy mire and thoroughly lost, that Edward even realised he had no idea where to search for a hibernating frog or toad. Should he be digging in the mud with his hands, or looking for mounds of leaf litter? Only brought out into the country for holidays, Edward knew little of the wildlife outside his home. He could no more recite the hibernation habits of a toad than he could tell a toad from a frog. Still, his brother had worked his way under his skin again, and Edward was determined not to return home until he had found a toad and presented it to Martin.

The further Edward ventured, the narrower and sparser the sections of dry, solid earth became. It felt like he was hop-stepping between little islands that poked out of the waters, and the frozen mud he had encountered on the edges of the wetlands had now turned wet and sludgy in these deeper recesses.

Mis-stepping twice more, Edward grumbled to himself as he hauled his left foot out of the boggy ground. The suction around his leg was incredible and he had to put real effort into pulling his leg free of the mire. He feared his boot being lost altogether and having to hop home on only one leg. However, when his leg became trapped a second time, his fears took on a more ominous turn.

As Edward's left leg sank up to his knee once more in the boggy swamp, he felt an even greater resistance as he tried to right himself. This time, he feared he was truly stuck in the mud and stranded all alone out on the fens. Panicked and yet still determined not to be defeated by the mire, Edward began to throw his whole weight this way and that, twisting his torso and reaching out to grab the roots of a nearby tree to use as an anchor as he attempted to free himself from the mud's wet clutches. He succeeded.

Throwing his weight all on one side and pulling on the tree root with all his might, Edward Stanford succeeded in hauling his leg out of the mire. However, the surprise of being free, and the lack of resistance against him, caused him to overbalance yet again. Thrown by the momentum and horribly unbalanced, Edward's body spanned over the narrow stretch of dry ground on which he stood. Time seemed to slow, and Edward seemed intensely aware of everything around him as he felt his balance tip and his whole body fall out into the deeper stretch of icy water on the farther side of him. He felt only momentary resistance against his back as the ice that frosted over the waters shattered around him. Then, all the boy knew was cold.

∼

Eliza had her skirts hiked up, mud and dirty water dirtying her stockings and boots as she plunged through the mists to get to the shadow that had fallen into the water. Ordinarily, she could navigate the bogs without getting a single stain on her, but when every second might be the difference between rescue and death, she had no time to check her footing. She had enough intuition and presence of mind to avoid the worst of the pitfalls, ensuring she did not become trapped in the mud as the stranger had done several times before finally falling into the waters.

As she neared the spot where the poor unfortunate soul had fallen Eliza was relieved to see she was well in time to perform a rescue. Though there was no sign of the man above the waterline, the water all about was frothing and swirling wildly as the stranger thrashed amongst the reeds and mud. Eliza breathed an urgent prayer for strength, and dropped down to her knees, hands reaching into the dark, murky waters and groping blindly until she felt something hard brush against her fingers. She seized it, relief filling her when she realised she had caught the stranger by the wrists. His fingers wrapped around hers and she began to pull, careful to keep her grip on the solid earth lest she be dragged down by the panicked, drowning man.

To Eliza's welcome surprise, the victim of the mires was not at all heavy and she was able to pull the figure out onto the banks with relative ease. It was only when he was halfway out of the water, coughing and spluttering for breath that she realised it was a boy near her own age. Realising this, Eliza worked all the harder to help the lad onto the shore, sacrificing her footing a little now she knew the boy's weight wouldn't threaten to drag her down into the water with him.

As the boy opened his eyes and took in much-needed lungsful of air, he seemed to become better aware of his surroundings, working with Eliza as he engaged his hands and knees and crawled onto the shore. At last, he was on dry land. He rolled onto his back, staring up into the sky and panting profusely as his mind processed the near-death experience.

"Are you all right? What happened to you? What are you doing out here on your own? Do you have a name?"

Eliza was a whirlwind of questions as she leaned over the boy, eyes wide with fright as she looked him over for injury...

∽

Who is this unfortunate victim of the mire? And what will come of this chance meeting? **Continue reading and delight yourself in this beautiful hope-filled tale...**

Continue Reading The Desperate Christmas Angel on Amazon

LOVE VICTORIAN CHRISTMAS SAGA ROMANCE?

If you enjoyed this story why not continue straight away with other books in our PureRead Victorian Christmas Romance library?

Read them all...

Churchyard Orphan

Orphan Christmas Miracle

Workhouse Girl's Christmas Dream

The Winter Widow's Daughter

The Match Girl & The Lost Boy's Christmas Hope

The Christmas Convent Child

The Orphan Girl's Winter Secret

Rag And Bone Winter Hope

Isadora's Christmas Plight

PLUS THESE BRAND NEW CHRISTMAS TALES
FROM OUR BESTSELLING VICTORIAN
ROMANCE AUTHORS

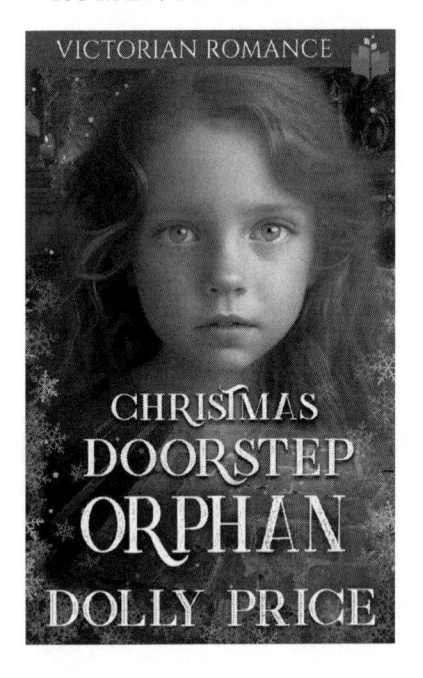

Read Christmas Doorstep Orphan on Amazon

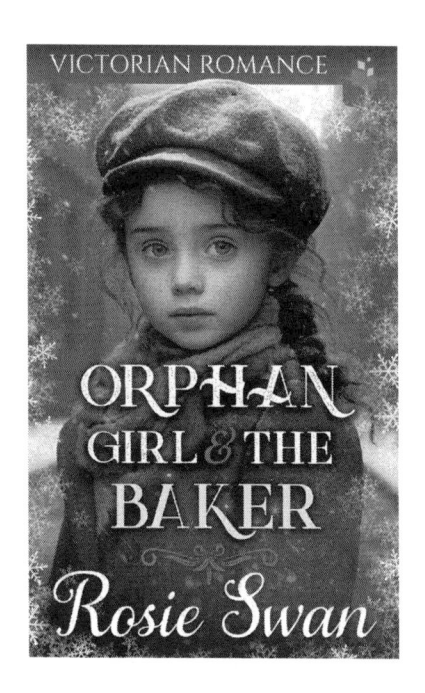

Read Orphan Girl & The Baker on Amazon

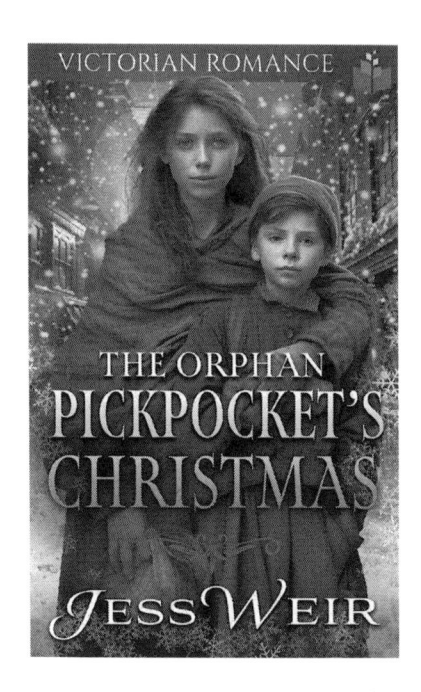

Read The Orphan Pickpocket's Christmas

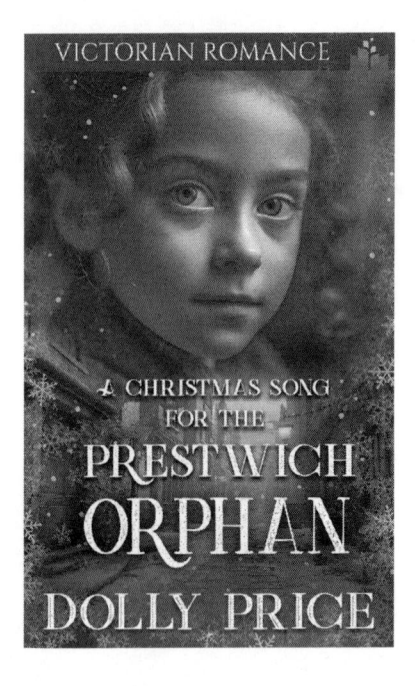

A Christmas Song For The Prestwich Orphan

OUR GIFT TO YOU

AS A WAY TO SAY THANK YOU WE WOULD LOVE TO SEND YOU THIS BEAUTIFUL STORY FREE OF CHARGE.

Click here for your free copy of Whitechapel Waif

PureRead.com/victorian

At PureRead we publish books you can trust. Great tales without smut or swearing, but with all of the mystery and romance you expect from a great story.

Be the first to know when we release new books, take part in our fun competitions, and get surprise free books in your inbox by signing up to our free VIP Reader list.

As a welcome gift you'll receive the story of the Whitechapel Waif straight to your inbox…

Click here for your free copy of Whitechapel Waif

PureRead.com/victorian

Printed in Great Britain
by Amazon